DEC   2002

W9-BGM-006

Playing the Field

Playing the Field

Janette Rallison

WALKER & COMPANY
NEW YORK

First published in the United States of America in 2002 by Walker Publishing Company, Inc.

Published simultaneously in Canada by Fitzhenry and Whiteside, Markham, Ontario L3R 4T8

For information about permission to reproduce selections from this book, write to Permissions, Walker & Company, 435 Hudson Street, New York, New York 10014

Library of Congress Cataloging-in-Publication Data

Rallison, Janette, 1966–
    Playing the field / Janette Rallison.
        p. cm.
    Summary: Thirteen-year-old McKay tries to keep up his algebra grade to stay on the baseball team, while dealing with his attraction to a girl named Serena.
    ISBN 0-8027-8804-1
    [1. Schools—Fiction. 2. Baseball—Fiction.] I. Title.

PZ7.R13455 P1   2001
[Fic]—dc21

                                        2001046981

Book design by Maura Rosenthal/mspaceny

Visit Walker & Company's Web site at www.walkerbooks.com

Printed in the United States of America

10 9 8 7 6 5 4 3 2 1

*T*o Mrs. Roberts's sixth-grade class, who critiqued the book for me and all loved it!

Stetson Anderson, Robbie Bates, Brittany Copeland, Stephanie Eason, Brendon Eastridge, Amy Flucker, Sarah Gilbert, Eric Gillispie, Melissa Gonzales, Ryan Infalt, Rhiannon Larosa, Brianna Lopez, Jared Moschcau, Evan Polson, Whitney Prince, Asenath Rallison (of course!), Lance Randall, Maryanna Reynolds—especially to Chris Rodriguez, who got hurt on his bike and told me, "I felt exactly like McKay"—Rebecca Rogers, Brittnee Scott, Heather Jarvis Serling, Greg Swerdan, Julio Tapia, Kristine Valenzuela, Chris Wallace, and Diana Wallace. Also thanks to Nathan Austin and Karissa Manwaring, who offered plot suggestions.

Thanks, guys!

Playing the Field

Mrs. Swenson was one of those teachers who probably got into the profession because she enjoyed making dour expressions. Her expression was especially dour when she gave me the news: "Mr. Conford, unless your test scores improve, and you start doing your homework, you're going to fail algebra."

Mrs. Swenson likes to call us by our last names. I guess it sounds more dour.

When my parents found out about my algebra grade, they used my first name. Repeatedly. With increased volume every time they said it.

"McKay, why haven't you been doing your homework?"

I had been doing it. I just hadn't been doing it right.

"McKay, why didn't you study for your last test?"

I did. Sort of. During the commercial breaks. I mean, it's October for heaven's sake, and the World Series is on.

"McKay, if you can't do the work right, you'll have to get a tutor and pay for it with your own money."

With the amount of allowance I got, I couldn't afford to hire anyone who actually knew more about algebra than I did. (By the way, I didn't actually say any of this, I just thought it. I may be failing algebra, but I'm not stupid.)

"McKay, if your grade hasn't improved at least to a C by the end of the quarter, you'll have to drop off the baseball team. That gives you just over a month to turn your grade around."

My parents know how to pack a threat. Granted, at the moment I was just playing fall ball. The regular season wouldn't start until spring, but baseball was a way of life for me, and I couldn't imagine not playing it. Besides, this year the league was having a districtwide fall ball tournament at the end of November, and my team was sure to win. I had to play.

I don't know why adults are so hung up on algebra, anyway. Why should I care what the letter x equals, when $4x + 7 + 8x = 43$? I have my life all figured out, and it doesn't involve algebra. I'm going to be a professional baseball player. All the math I'll need to know is how to add runs, how to average batting scores, and of course, how to calculate interest on all of the money I'll make. I don't care which train reaches Philadelphia first—the one leaving from New York and traveling 55 m.p.h. or the one leaving from Washington, D.C., going 40 m.p.h. I live in Gilbert, Arizona. When I'm a professional ballplayer and do start to travel, I'm going to use a private jet.

I've tried to explain this to Mrs. Swenson. On the last test when she asked one of those stupid train questions, I wrote,

"Professional ballplayers let their managers worry about their travel schedules."

Mrs. Swenson has no sense of humor. When I'm famous, I'm never going to autograph a baseball for her.

That night I sat down at the kitchen table and tried to do the next day's assignment. I wrote $2x^2 + 12x = -18$ neatly on my piece of paper. Then I stared at the mysterious x for a while, hoping it would give me some hint as to its identity. I tried to remember how Mrs. Swenson had explained these problems to the class, but I hadn't been listening carefully, so I didn't get very far.

When Mom walked by, I asked her if she could help me figure it out. She sat down next to me at the table and picked up the book. She scanned over the equations and then said, "It's been a long time since I've done this type of math problem." She tapped my pencil against the table, then wrote down some numbers. "Let's see, I think you're supposed to divide both sides of the equation by twelve, wait, that's not it. . . ." She wrote down a few more numbers, then scribbled them out.

"Just wait till they put those equations on trains and send them off to Philadelphia," I told her.

She laid down the pencil and said, "Maybe your father will remember how to do this stuff."

We looked at one another silently for a moment. Dad is the one who refuses to balance the checkbook because he can't get his figures to match the bank's. He sits at the kitchen table,

◇

shaking his head at the bank statement, and insists that the bank has messed up again and computers can't be trusted.

Mom let out a sigh. "Or maybe we really are going to have to get you a tutor."

I pulled my paper back in front of me and stared down at it with determination. "I don't need a tutor." My allowance doesn't even cover the cost of decently updating my baseball card collection. The last thing I wanted was another expense. "I'll call Tony and see if he knows how to do this."

Mom raised an eyebrow. Tony is my best friend, but not the best at algebra. "Isn't there someone else in your class you could ask?"

"I'll ask Tony first."

"Well, don't spend too long on the phone. Remember, you don't do anything with friends until your homework is done."

"I know, I know." I picked up my math book and trudged over to the phone. I bet Cal Ripkin Jr.'s mother had never given him these types of lectures when he was growing up.

Tony tried to explain the assignment to me, but it still didn't make a lot of sense. I just couldn't get some of the equations to work out. Instead of my trains meeting anywhere, I think they both got derailed in hideous wrecks.

My dad wasn't much more help when he got home. Before bed he looked over my algebra problems, but it was really only a symbolic gesture. It was only because my mom made him. He held my paper up and got a studious look on his face. "Well. Yes. I see. Very interesting." He put the paper down and nodded,

"It's nice to know some things never change. After all these years, we're still searching for the meaning of *x*."

My mom glared at him, but he ignored her and leaned closer to me. "This is exactly the reason I became a plumber."

Mom said, "Bill, you're not helping."

"Well, I would if he ever brought home assignments about installing water lines."

In a lower tone Mom told him, "United we stand, divided we get kid-sized footprints on our faces."

"Uh, right," Dad said. Then he patted my shoulder. "Do your algebra, go to college, and become an aerospace engineer."

Mom rolled her eyes. "If you're not being serious with McKay now, how do you expect him to take us seriously when we tell him he has to pass algebra or quit baseball?"

Dad said, "I told him to do his algebra. What's not serious about that?"

"I think I understand it now," I said because I hate it when my parents fight.

Mom looked at me skeptically. "You understand it now?"

"Yeah. Tony did a good job of explaining it to me. See. I finished all of the problems." I picked up my paper and showed it to her.

She looked it over. "*X* equals 5.342? Shouldn't *x* be a whole number like 7 or 12 or something?"

"Not necessarily," I said.

How could she argue the point? After all, she didn't know how to do the problems any more than I did.

She handed me back the paper. "All right."

"See," Dad said. "He's on his way to engineering school right now."

Mom didn't say anything more, and she left the kitchen.

Dad watched her leave, then said, "I don't think she likes engineers. Maybe you'd better become a brain surgeon instead."

The next day at school when we went over the assignment in class, I got thirteen out of twenty right. That's only 65 percent. I may not be great at algebra, but I've been figuring out percentages since I could read the back of a baseball card. Sixty-five percent was a D. Not exactly the kind of grade that would get me into medical school or keep me on the baseball team.

I felt sick for the rest of class. This time I'd really tried to do the homework, and I had still failed. All through lunch I kept saying, "I'm doomed. My baseball career is over."

"No, it's not," Tony said. "You'll get a tutor, and you'll be fine."

"I'm doomed, and my allowance will be gone," I said.

"Maybe you could get someone at school to help you for free."

"You helped me, and I only got twelve problems right."

"Someone who's better at math than I am." Tony nodded toward the other side of the cafeteria, where Serena Kimball sat.

Serena was good at math. In fact, Serena was good at everything. She was not only a straight-A student, but she was also the vice president of the eighth grade. Every year, while the teachers looked on in admiration, she played a piano concerto for the school talent show. In all the years I'd gone to school with her, I'd never once seen her long brown hair out of place.

"Right," I said. "I'll just waltz up to her and ask her if she'd like to come home with me and run some equations."

"You could at least talk to her. You know, be friendly. Chat about things. Then when you mention you're having a hard time with your math, if she likes you, she'll volunteer to help you."

"If she likes me?" I asked. "Why would she like me?"

"Why not?" Tony said. "If you tried, you could be"—he waved his hand over me like he was performing a magic trick— "hunk material."

I picked up my empty sandwich bag, crumpled it up, and threw it at him.

Tony had shown an increased interest in girls since we'd entered the eighth grade, but I still thought of them as odd creatures who couldn't throw a ball the right way and always went to the bathroom in packs. Oh, sure, there had been Stephanie Morris in kindergarten—we held hands during recess, and she told me she wanted to marry me. But after a couple of weeks of us walking around like a small paper-doll chain, she said she'd decided to marry Randall Parker instead. No explanation. She led Randall around the playground for the next few weeks until she got tired of him, and then she started holding hands with Bobby Friedman.

◇

That's when I decided girls were more trouble than they were worth.

Still, I looked over at Serena. She was leaning across the table and telling her friend, Rachel, something. Both of their faces were animated and laughing. The end of Serena's hair brushed against the table, and her face tilted sideways like she was about to tell Rachel a secret. I tried to imagine Serena sitting at my kitchen table, talking and laughing like that. Somehow it just didn't seem likely.

Tony nudged me again. "Serena would be tons better than a paid tutor. Don't you remember that tutor my sister got for her French class? It was some college student who spit when he talked and smelled funny. You don't want to pay some guy to come over to your house and spit at you, do you?" He nodded toward Serena again. "Trust me, Serena's the way to go. You just have to think of some casual way to talk to her."

"Like what?"

"You know, go up to her and say something."

I looked from Serena back to Tony. "Like what?"

Tony wadded up his lunch sack and made a hook shot into the garbage can. "Don't you know anything about girls?" When I looked at him blankly, he said, "It's a game. The next best game after baseball. Only instead of a bat to get on base, you use your words and dashing smile."

I gave him my most skeptical look.

"Watch a master at work. I'm about to turn on the old Manetti charm."

Ever since Tony had noticed girls, he'd been drawing upon his Italian heritage to help him radiate charm. He was also working on what he called a "cool walk." It was sort of a cross between a rooster strut and a cowboy swagger, although sometimes when he didn't coordinate it right, it looked like he had something stuck on the bottom of his shoes, and he was trying to scrape it off. Now he walked up to Serena's table doing the cool walk, and his strut and his swagger were almost perfectly timed. I followed him with my hands shoved into my pockets.

"Hi, Rachel. Hi, Serena." He stopped a couple of feet away from them. "What are you guys doing?"

Rachel and Serena glanced at each other, then looked back at us with somewhat puzzled expressions. "We're eating lunch," Rachel said.

"Right," Tony said. "We just finished."

"Oh," Serena said.

I gulped and swallowed, and mostly looked at Serena's shoes.

"The lunch was pretty good today," Tony said.

"Oh, really?" Rachel said. "We brought sack lunches."

So had we. I was glad the girls didn't know this little fact, as they would have thought we were total idiots. As it was now, we might be able to escape this situation with the girls only thinking we were partial idiots.

"Yeah," Tony said. "Lunch was good."

The girls nodded at us with the same patronizing stare you use when you're talking to four-year-olds.

"I guess we'll be going now," Tony said.

"Okay," Rachel said.

As we turned and walked to the door, I could hear the girls erupt into giggles. I was glad my back was to them so they couldn't see my face turn red. I shook my head at Tony and said, "That was a master at work?"

"It was a start," Tony said.

"I think it was a strikeout."

Tony pushed the cafeteria door open with more force than he needed to. "It was breaking the ice. Now it will be easier to talk to them next time."

"Next time?" Even though we were out of the cafeteria, I could still hear Serena and Rachel's laughter in my mind. I shook my head again, and walked a little faster. "I think I'd rather pay all of my allowance to have some funny-smelling college student come over and spit at me."

After school, on the days we had baseball practice, I always walked home with Tony. His dad then drove us to the baseball field for practice. Mr. Manetti was the coach of the Gilbert Coyotes, the best team in the East Valley League; that's how Tony and I originally became friends. We were on the same team in fourth grade and have played ball together ever since. Tony plays third base. I'm on second. We have our system down pat. I can field a ball and deliver it to Tony before the base runners even know where it's at. We call the space between second and third "no-man's-land," and we let no man cross it without feeling our wrath.

Tony's dad is a realtor, but I think his real passion is baseball. He was an all-star in college and even had an offer from the Angels to play on their farm team, but he decided realty was a more stable profession, so he'd followed that instead. Sometimes I wondered if he regretted the decision, though. For someone who'd rather be selling houses than playing ball, he sure spent an awful lot of time on the baseball diamond.

As we were fixing ourselves a snack in the kitchen, Tony's older sister, Jenna, came in and sat down at the table. Her dark hair was twisted up in curlers, and she held her head perfectly straight so as not to jiggle them. She opened a bottle of finger-nail polish and began painting her nails light purple. In between painting them, she blew on them.

After she was done with one hand, she looked over at Tony and said, "I'm seeing Adam tonight. I'll need your help again."

Tony and I had just finished off half a bag of potato chips, and now he grabbed the peanut butter from the cupboard. "I'm busy eating."

"You can talk and eat at the same time," she said. "You do it all of the time."

Tony opened a package of bread and handed me a couple of pieces. "Adam is into baseball," he told me. "So now Jenna wants to be an expert."

She held up her hands and examined her nails. "How com-plicated can it be? You play it all of the time."

Tony ignored her and got the jam from the refrigerator. Jenna turned to me. "You're a walking baseball encyclopedia like my brother. You tell me something."

"Like what?"

"Like who was the best ever pitcher?"

"Cy Young," I said.

"Nolan Ryan," Tony said.

"Make up your minds and tell me why."

"His pitching record," I said.

"Because he throws with style," Tony said.

Jenna shook her head. "Are we talking about Young or Ryan?"

"Yes," we both answered at once.

"Oh, never mind," Jenna rolled her eyes and sighed. "Tell me about both of them."

We gave her statistics for both Young and Ryan, and she repeated them as though she were trying to memorize a foreign language.

Tony finished off one sandwich then got out bread to make another. "How could you have lived with Dad and me for so long and know so little about baseball?"

"It's been hard," she said, "but I've gotten pretty good at tuning the two of you out."

"Thanks."

Jenna shrugged. "Well, I can't help it if I don't like baseball. I mean you hit a ball with a stick. How interesting is that?"

Tony gave her a long look. "Why don't you just give up now and tell Adam you know nothing about the sport?"

"Because he's the best-looking guy in the junior class. Maybe in the whole school."

"You can't just fake that you're a baseball fan forever."

"Yes, I can." She got a dreamy look in her eyes and slowly smiled. "For Adam, I can."

Tony looked over at me. "What did I expect her to say? We're talking about someone who streaks her hair, puts on makeup to get the mail, and wears shoes that make her look an inch taller."

"Oh," she replied tartly. "And I suppose the reason you've been lifting weights lately is because the barbells need to be elevated several times a day. It airs them out."

Tony blushed. "Lifting weights helps my batting technique."

"Right," she said. "As in, you want a bunch of girls to bat their eyes at you."

"A lot of baseball players lift weights," Tony insisted. "We also jog."

"Oh, really?" Jenna's voice sounded studious again. "What else do you have to do?"

We told her what went on at practice, but in the end she decided to come with us to watch. She also took paper and pencil so she could take notes. Then while we played, she sat in the bleachers, pencil poised, and observed us.

It made practice that much harder. Every time I messed up, I wondered if Jenna was jotting it down. Later on she'd corner me somewhere and ask, "So, when you hit a ball straight up in the air and the pitcher runs up and catches it, are you *supposed* to drop to your knees and scream, or is that just your own personal ritual?"

Usually I'm a great batter. My average is .410.

I tried to ignore Jenna the best I could.

As Tony and I walked on the field to toss long balls, Tony brought up the subject of Serena again. "We walk by her locker on the way to math class. Tomorrow we should, you know, stop by and talk with her."

"What exactly would we talk about?" This was always my problem when it came to girls. What did you say to them? With guys it was easy. You could say anything to a guy and not worry about it. Even if you said the most stupid thing in the world, he wouldn't care. He wouldn't make a big deal about it and sit around with his other friends giggling about you. Now I'm not saying absolutely that this is what girls do. But if they're not laughing about boys, why is it you always see them huddled in groups, and they giggle as certain boys walk by?

Tony shrugged. "We could talk about math class. You know, you could say, 'Hey, Serena, did you finish all your math homework? That Mrs. Swenson is such a slave driver. She never gives us a free moment, does she?'"

That didn't seem too hard to say, except when I pictured myself walking up to Serena's locker and actually saying any of it. I mean, I know by the time boys are in the eighth grade they're not supposed to be afraid to talk to girls, and a lot of my friends weren't. Tony wasn't. But Tony isn't me. He has that "old Manetti charm" working for him.

I looked skeptically at Tony. "You don't think she'll think I'm a loser?"

"Naw. Why would she? We'll just talk to her. Lots of people talk to each other. It's no big deal. But remember, you've got to say something this time. Otherwise she'll think *I* like her, and where would that leave you?"

"Peacefully sitting in algebra class enjoying my dignity."

"Peacefully flunking your algebra class," Tony said.

I opened and closed my glove a few times in an attempt to loosen it up. "All right. Tomorrow I'll talk to her."

Tomorrow came much sooner than I would have liked. First, second, and third period also went too fast, and then I was walking down the hall with Tony toward Serena's locker.

I thought about trying to imitate Tony's cool walk, but I figured I'd better practice in front of a mirror before I undertook anything so major. Instead, I grabbed my math book as hard as I could while still trying to look casual.

"What do you think about Rachel and me?" Tony asked me as we walked.

"Rachel and you what?"

He rolled his eyes. "You know, Rachel and me as a couple."

"Do you even know Rachel?"

"Sure." Tony smiled a little. "I've seen her around. She's cute."

I slowed down a bit because we were coming up to Serena's locker, and suddenly it was all I could do to drag my feet across the floor. "Yeah, but do you know anything about Rachel?"

"I know she's Serena's friend. Just think, if you become a couple, and Rachel and I become a couple, we could do things together."

"We don't need girls to do things together. We do things

together all the time. Like right now we're about to go make total fools of ourselves together."

"Speak for yourself," Tony said.

I took a swing at him with my math book but missed. I was thinking of some really good insult to fling back at him, but we'd reached Serena's locker. She was kneeling down to get something at the bottom, and Rachel was leaning against the next locker over, waiting for her.

I had never seen the inside of Serena's locker, but I should have guessed it would be spotlessly clean. All of her books stood neatly stacked across the shelf, and there were no crumpled papers littering it up like there were in mine. She even had pictures of horses taped to the door. In my locker there's nothing on the door but the wadded-up gum someone stuck there last year that I've never bothered to clean off.

Serena looked up at me, and I cleared my throat. I tried to remember what it was Tony said I should say, but somehow under the pressure of her gaze I forgot the first part of my speech. Instead of saying, "Hey, Serena, did you finish all of your math homework? That Mrs. Swenson, what a slave driver. She never gives us a free moment," I just croaked out, "Hi, Serena, we never get a free moment, do we?"

Her jaw dropped a little, like she couldn't believe I'd said that—which made two of us, since I couldn't believe it either. With one hand still in her locker she said, "A free moment to do what?"

◇

"Algebra," I said quickly. "There's never a free moment to do algebra."

"Oh." She nodded slightly and stood up. "I did my assignment last night. Didn't you get it done?"

"Oh, sure, I did it. I'm just not certain I did it right." Tony hadn't told me what I was supposed to talk about after my first statement, and suddenly I felt myself grasping for anything to say. "You know, I always think x equals one thing, and Mrs. Swenson has other ideas. That's the problem with math. There's no room for different opinions." Out of the corner of my eye I saw Tony shake his head, but I plunged on anyway. "And why do you think they use the letter x so much in math anyway? We hardly ever use it in English class. I mean, how many words can you think of that start with x?"

"Xylophone," Serena said.

"Exactly my point," I said. "How often do you use the word *xylophone*?"

Serena and Rachel walked toward the math classroom, and Tony and I followed them, and although I hate to admit it, I was still spouting off my feelings about the letter x to her all the way down the hallway. "You see, it's a difficult letter," I told her as we walked through Mrs. Swenson's door. "And that's why they use it in math class. Math teachers want these problems to be hard."

"Uh-huh." Serena smiled at me before she took her seat, but I'm not sure whether it was the kind of smile that meant, I think you're nice, or whether it was the kind of smile that meant, Which of your multiple personalities was I just speaking to?

I sat down sullenly in my own seat and opened my book to our assignment page. Tony sat down in the next row over. He was still shaking his head.

I tore a piece of notebook paper out and wrote, "I talked about math class to her. I thought you said she'd offer to help me."

While Mrs. Swenson wrote equations on the board, I passed the note to Tony. He read it, wrote his reply, and passed it back to me. It said, "With your speech on the letter x, it's amazing the school counselor doesn't offer to help you. Besides, this was the first time you ever talked to her. Give it some time. Say hello to her a few more times."

I made myself listen to every word Mrs. Swenson had to say during her next algebra explanation. I hoped that if I listened this time instead of doodling pictures of baseball stadiums on my notebook, then suddenly everything would make sense. But it didn't. And the worst part of it was, I knew it was my own fault. If I had paid attention from the beginning, if I'd asked for help when it first got hard, I wouldn't have these problems now.

I scanned the room looking for someone else who might be willing to help me out. Brett Parson? He thought he was too good for everyone. He probably wouldn't slow down in the hall long enough to say hello to me, let alone spend time with me and a math book. Rich Shefler? He'd been mad at me since that basketball game when he'd been hogging the ball, so I refused to throw it to him no matter how open he was. Ian Thompson? I didn't know him that well, but maybe . . .

As I looked around the room, I caught Serena's eye. She smiled at me, then turned back toward Mrs. Swenson.

Or maybe, I thought, maybe Serena wasn't such a bad choice after all.

When I got home from school, the first thing I noticed was that my little brother, Kirk, had gotten into my dresser and dumped my clothes all over the floor. I put my backpack on my bed and went to find the little shrimpola.

I was an only child for eight years before Kirk came along, and to tell you the truth, I didn't appreciate my onlyness. My parents had tried to have more children for years but weren't able to. They'd just decided we were stuck being a three-person family, then Kirk surprised us all. When my parents told me I was going to have a brother, I was so happy I went wild. That was five years ago, before I realized a little brother's main purpose in life is getting into his big brother's stuff.

I walked into the family room and found Kirk watching TV, wearing only my underwear. "Kirk, what are you doing?"

"Watching my Pokémon video," he said.

"I mean," I said a bit more forcefully. "What are you doing in my underwear?"

"Watching Pokémon," he said again.

I went and stood in front of the TV. "Number one, you're not supposed to get into my dresser. Number two, you left all of my clothes on the floor, and number three, you're not allowed to wear my things."

He stood up and put his hands on his hips. "Get out of my way, or I'll tell Mom."

"I'm not moving until you put my clothes back in my dresser and get out of my underwear."

Kirk tried to push me away, using moves he no doubt learned from Pokémon's Team Rocket. Luckily, I'm a little more difficult to vanquish. I put my hand on his head and held him away until he got so frustrated he yelled for Mom.

Mom came into the room two seconds later and looked at me accusingly. "You can't even be home for five minutes without fighting with your brother?"

I let go of Kirk but didn't step out of the way. "He dumped all of my clothes on the floor, and he's wearing my underwear."

Now Mom's gaze turned to my brother. "Kirk?"

"I spilled milk on myself and got all soaked, and I didn't have any clean underwear."

Mom sighed, mumbled something about doing the laundry, then said, "Go pick up McKay's clothes and put them back in his dresser."

"And my underwear?" I asked.

"It won't kill you to let him borrow your underwear."

"But Mom—"

"You're not using them right now, and he needs some."

This just goes to show you how unreasonable mothers can be. After all, a guy's underwear ought to be sacred. I mean, what if somebody came over and saw those size-16 briefs hanging off Kirk's skinny little body? They'd know they were getting a firsthand look at my private matters.

Kirk gave me a smug look and left the room.

"Put them all back in the right drawers!" I called after him. Then I followed Mom into the laundry room.

"I have got to have my own room," I told her. It was a matter we'd discussed before, but Mom always used one of three excuses to tell me I had to stay put: (1) It's too much work to move somebody out; (2) Kirk will be lonely without you; (3) We don't have the room.

We have a three-bedroom house, and the smallest bedroom is used as an office. My mom works at home as a medical transcriptionist, so she needs a computer, a filing cabinet, and that sort of stuff. In addition, she has every sewing project and craft she ever planned to finish stuffed into the closet. It's probably the most crowded room in the house, but to my way of thinking, where there's a will, there's a way to get Kirk out of my room.

This time Mom started out with excuse number three. "We don't have the room for separate bedrooms in this house."

"Then let's get a bigger house."

"We've gone over this before. We don't have the money for a bigger house yet."

"Well, when is 'yet' ever going to happen?"

"Either when you and Kirk stop outgrowing your clothes on a monthly basis, or when Daddy or I get a raise." She picked out some whites from the laundry basket and threw them into the washer. "Neither of which," she muttered, "is likely to happen soon."

I leaned against the dryer. "Couldn't you just move your desk and all that office stuff into your bedroom?"

Mom threw a few more clothes into the washer. "You know how early your dad gets up. If we had the computer in our room, then I couldn't work on things at night because he'd be sleeping. Besides, I'm not sure all of that stuff would fit into our room."

"But Kirk constantly gets into my things. He has no respect for my property."

Mom sighed. "I'll talk to him about it."

"When my friends come over, we can't hang out in my room because he always follows us in there."

"He looks up to you," Mom said.

"I'd like him to look up to me from a different bedroom."

Mom dumped some soap in the machine and turned the dial slowly. "I'll discuss it with your father."

This was farther than I'd ever gotten before on issue number three, and I said, "Really?"

Mom shut the lid of the washer and picked up stray socks on the floor. "Right now it's just talking."

"Right," I said. But after Mom left the room I did a little victory dance anyway.

When my dad came home from work, I was a model child. I complimented him on how clean he kept his truck. I got him the mail. I even made Herculean efforts not to fight with Kirk.

When dinner came, I remembered to say please and thank you as the food was passed around. Then I asked him how his day had gone.

"My truck, the mail, and now my day, huh?" He nodded at me knowingly. "You're in some sort of trouble, aren't you?"

I put my hand across my chest as though I'd been wounded. "Not at all. I'm just trying to be the thoughtful kind of person you've raised me to be."

Mom rolled her eyes but didn't contradict me.

Dad broke a roll in half and spread margarine on one side. "My day . . ." He took a bite of his roll and seemed to contemplate this for a while. "I took a shower halfway apart trying to find a leak, and then I fixed a couple of toilets—had to take one of them all the way off, and then I spent nearly two hours installing a reverse osmosis system. It was the most annoying piece of equipment I've come across in a long time, and the worst thing is it was our own RO system."

The water in Arizona has roughly the same aftertaste as cough syrup, so most people either buy bottled water or filter their water through an RO system.

"Hendricks Plumbing has their own RO systems?" I asked.

"They do now. About a month ago they bought out a local RO company. So now not only do I have to install the stupid things, I'm supposed to be pushing them too."

"Sounds like hard work," I said. "Any chance you'll be getting a raise soon?"

Dad guffawed. "You know what Mr. Hendricks told us at our last general meeting? He said we give ourselves our own raises now—through commission sales. Every time I recommend a Hendricks system and someone buys it, I get a two-hundred-dollar bonus."

"Well that's a good thing, isn't it?"

"I'm a plumber, not a salesman. I'm not about to go pushing RO systems. Honestly, what does Hendricks expect us to say to people? 'I'm here to unclog your sink, and by the way, have you ever considered the advantages of purified water?'"

Dad and Mom then discussed several other faults Mr. Hendricks had, including, but not limited to, the fact that he tried to get out of paying overtime. But I wasn't listening anymore. I was trying to calculate how many systems Dad would need to sell in order to pay the mortgage on a four-bedroom house. How much extra a month did bigger houses cost? Two hundred dollars? Three hundred perhaps? My parents had never discussed the mortgage payment with me, but certainly four hundred dollars a month ought to pay for another bedroom. That meant my dad would only have to consistently sell two ROs a month. Selling two a month didn't sound that hard.

True, my dad had just said he didn't want to be a salesman, but then probably no one wants to be a salesman in the beginning. It's something people just do because they have to.

Last summer I'd gone door-to-door and sold newspaper

subscriptions to earn funds for baseball camp. At first I'd felt awkward ringing doorbells. I'd been afraid people would be mad at me for interrupting them. But after a while I realized it wasn't so scary. Most everybody was nice, and some people actually wanted to buy the paper. I made enough money to go to camp. If I, a thirteen-year-old boy who didn't actually read the newspaper, could sell them, then certainly my dad, a water expert, could sell some ROs. All I had to do was convince him he'd be successful.

Between bites of spaghetti, I looked over at him and said, "I think you'd be a great salesman, Dad. I mean, if I were a stranger and you told me about Hendricks ROs, I'd buy one from you."

"Yeah, and I keep my truck very tidy too. Flattery will get you nowhere, McKay, I'm onto you."

"No, I mean it."

He cocked his head and folded his arms across his chest. "Just get it over with and tell me what you want. The suspense is killing me."

Mom said, "McKay and I were talking this afternoon about moving my work stuff into our room and making the office into a bedroom. I think that's what all these compliments are about." Then she looked over at me and said, "How come you never told me my car was tidy before you hit me up for a new room?"

"Hmm," Dad said, and it wasn't a very enthusiastic *hmm*.

Mom said, "The boys *are* a little old to share a room."

"I shared a room with my brother till I moved out of the house," Dad said.

She smiled over at him. "Yes, but if you remember, you didn't like that arrangement."

"I also don't like turning my bedroom into an office."

Kirk must have finally realized what the conversation was about because he suddenly piped in with, "Is McKay leaving our bedroom?"

"No," I said. "You're leaving."

"Uh-uh," he said.

"Yes-huh," I said.

Mom gave us a stern look. "I think your father and I will discuss it later by ourselves."

"And I can tell you right now," Dad said, pointing at me, "if you want to convince me to turn my bedroom into medical transcription central, then you'd better not let up on that flattery for weeks, maybe months."

"You're the perfect dad," I said.

"You're darn right I am," he said and went back to his dinner.

I was in a great mood for the rest of the evening—that is, I was in a great mood until I sat down to do my homework. I diagrammed sentences for my English class, I read about Jamestown for history—and then I stared at my math problems. Not only had x shown up again for today's assignment, but he'd brought y along with him too. They were both in disguise, and I was supposed to figure out which numbers they really were. Thirteen? Fifty-four? Sixty-nine and a half? They weren't telling, and I had no way to know.

I hadn't even gotten the x equations figured out, and already the assignments were getting harder. I wondered how many letters Mrs. Swenson planned on adding to our math class and how far behind I'd be by the time we'd gone through the whole alphabet. I flipped through the book and thought about waiting until tomorrow morning to do the assignment. Then I thought about baseball and keeping my parents happy, and plunged into the assignment anyway.

It didn't go very well. I was able to do the first problem but wasn't sure I'd done it right. Could x actually equal $2y$? Was that a legitimate answer? I mean, that only limited the value of x to somewhere between infinity and negative infinity.

Wasn't Mrs. Swenson looking for something a little more specific?

Hmm.

Perhaps I could convince my parents that you didn't need to know algebra to become a brain surgeon.

I did the rest of the problems, then called Tony to check my answers with his. We got different answers for six of the fifteen problems. Tony was sure he'd done his right because Jenna had helped him, so I decided to bike over to his house so he could show me how he'd done them.

After I got there, I looked over Tony's answers and decided to cross Jenna off the Possible Tutors list.

I pointed to one of Tony's problems. "Look at this factor," I said. "It can't possibly be right. X can't equal $2x$. That's like saying 3 equals 6."

Tony picked up his paper. "Dang. You're right. I wonder why Jenna didn't catch that?" He looked at it a moment longer and muttered, "She was probably too busy lotioning up her cuticles to notice." He shoved the paper back into his notebook and shrugged. "Oh, well. I'll just ask her about it when she gets home from her date. Let's get something to eat."

I followed him into the kitchen glumly. How could he be so unworried about it? I watched him open cupboards and said, "Your parents don't want you to be a brain surgeon, do they?"

"I'll probably be a realtor like my dad. He says he can teach me all the secrets to sell homes."

"There are secrets?"

"Sure."

Tony was probably right because the Manettis seemed to have lots of money. They lived in a big house with nice furniture, and had both a BMW and a Silverado to drive.

I wondered if there were secrets to selling ROs, and if so, who knew them.

Tony took a box of Ding Dongs from a cupboard and threw me one. "I can call you after Jenna gets in and helps me with that problem, but it might be late. She's out with Adam the Wonderful."

I caught the Ding Dong and ripped off the wrapper. "She's actually pulling off that whole being-a-baseball-fan thing?"

"I guess so, because she's still drilling me with baseball questions every night."

I bit my Ding Dong in half and squeezed out some of the

cream filling. "Man, that Adam guy must be totally clueless if he hasn't figured out by now she's just pretending to know baseball."

"Naw. Pretending is regular for dating. It's part of playing the game. Everyone does it."

"Cool. I'm going to pretend to be Cal Ripkin then."

"No, I'm serious." Tony went into the family room and picked up a magazine off the couch. The cover said *Teen Spirit* and showed a beautiful teenage girl with long blond hair and a big smile. "This is one of Jenna's How-to-Pretend-to-Be-Someone-Else manuals." He opened to the table of contents, and then put his half-eaten Ding Dong on the countertop. Reading out loud, he said, "Three easy steps to getting his attention . . . Be thinner by Thursday . . . Clothes that erase flaws. And then of course there's the makeup feature." He flipped a few pages to that section. I looked at the before and after pictures with my mouth hanging half open.

"That's what girls go through to put on makeup?"

"Scary, isn't it. You should see Jenna after she gets up in the morning."

Tony looked over at the next page. "Hey, this looks interesting. Does your boyfriend have the right stuff?"

I shoved the last piece of my Ding Dong into my mouth. "What's so interesting about that?"

A mischievous smile came across his face. "It's a cheat sheet for what girls are looking for in a guy." He pointed to the article. "Look, on this side we have the qualities of Mr. Right, and over here we have qualities of Mr. Ought-to-Be Left-in-the-Dust." He shook his head as he read over the last column. "Apparently girls don't like guys who are jealous or cheap."

I went to the fridge and poured milk for Tony and myself while he scanned over the rest of the article. When I was done, I handed him his glass, but he set it down on the counter instead of drinking it.

Finally he nodded confidently. "Okay. I think I could pass for Mr. Right." He cleared his throat as he looked at the magazine. "Number one, I'm supposed to have a good sense of humor." He held the magazine down for a moment. "People are always telling me I'm funny."

"Yeah, but I don't think they're talking about your sense of humor."

He ignored me. "Number two. I'm supposed to be honest. I could fake that."

"Uh, wouldn't that be dishonest?"

He still ignored me. "Number three. Attractive." He held the magazine to the side for a moment and swept one hand in front of himself. "Need I say more?"

I rolled my eyes.

"Number four. Loyal. Of course that's me. After all, I was a Boy Scout, and Boy Scouts are always loyal, brave, and trustworthy."

"Yeah, I bet girls will be really impressed with your scouting background. You can tell them about the time you cut up bugs to do your insect-study merit badge, Mr. Right."

"And lastly, I'm supposed to be understanding." He laid the magazine on the countertop. "That's the only one I'm going to have to work on." He picked up the rest of his Ding Dong and ate it while he contemplated this. "I think from now on, when I'm talking to girls I'll nod every once in a while and say, 'I understand.'"

"That'll make you irresistible."

He grinned and said, "I can hardly wait to try this out." For a moment he pretended he was talking to someone. "Really, Rachel? I understand." He nodded slowly and said, "I *honestly* understand."

"You loyally, humorously, attractively understand."

Tony picked up his drink of milk and took a swallow. "Go ahead and laugh now. We'll see who's laughing after it works."

"It'll never work."

"I dare you to try it out on Serena."

I folded my arms. "I don't even talk to Serena. How would I convince her I'm loyal?"

"That's just the point, McKay. You've got to talk to her."

I knew he was right, but I didn't like it. I finished off my milk and glanced back at the kitchen table, where our assignments lay. "I suppose I can just say hi to her a few more times and see what happens." That somehow didn't seem quite so bad.

4

Over the next two days I said hello to Serena four times. I don't even say hello that often to some of my friends. Once, when I ran into Serena on the way to math class, I complimented her on the tidiness of her locker. Then while we walked to the room, we had a two-minute conversation about horses because I mentioned the pictures she had hung on her locker door. She told me they were her aunt's horses, but she gets to ride them whenever her family visits her aunt's ranch in Texas. One was a "paint," and one was something else. They both looked spotted brown to me, but I nodded approvingly anyway.

"I understand," I said.

She blinked at me. "You understand what?"

I could only think of one thing to understand, so I said, "I, uh, understand why you like to ride horses."

"You like to ride too?"

Well, I didn't dislike it, and besides, I couldn't very well say no after I'd just told her I understood why she liked to ride horses. "Yeah," I said, "I really like horseback riding."

"Cool. Where do you usually go?"

Whatever I said next would undoubtedly disqualify me as Mr. Right due to that honesty clause. "The mountains," I said.

She nodded. "That's fun, but I like riding out on flat land the best. That way your horse can run."

"I understand," I said again.

After I sat down at my desk in algebra class, Tony passed me a note. It read, "I saw you walk in with Serena. Anything happen?"

I'm not sure what he meant by "anything," but from the smirk on his face he must have been referring to the rockets of our love igniting. I wrote back, "I found out her aunt has horses."

Tony sent the note back with "Is she being friendly to you?" scribbled on it.

I wrote, "I don't know. I've noticed she and Rachel giggle a lot when I walk by now," then handed the note across the aisle to him.

He made a big production of blowing kisses at me and wrote, "She must like you. You must like her." As I read the note he whispered across the aisle, "Will you name your first son after me, since I suggested you get together?"

I wanted to lean over and punch him. Instead I wrote, "I don't like her. I just want her to help me with my math."

Tony wrote back, "You're such a baby, McKay. It's okay to like girls. They don't actually have cooties, you know."

I would have written something back to him, something insulting to put him in his place, but Mrs. Swenson walked down the aisle just then, so I shoved the paper into my math folder instead.

I wasn't a baby, and I liked girls. I even liked Serena a little. But I don't know. I couldn't explain it; not to Tony, and not even to myself. It was like the time when I was in third grade and I had a part in our class play. I played a Spanish explorer in early America. I was supposed to come onto the stage, turn to the audience, and say, "There's gold in America. We'll strike it rich in the new land!" I never had problems with my part during the rehearsal. I knew every word of my lines. I drove my parents crazy by saying them at least fifteen times during every meal.

Then the day of the play came. All of our parents crowded into the school auditorium carrying cameras and video recorders. I stood backstage wearing my tinfoil conquistador's hat and was so excited I was jumping up and down. When it was my turn, I walked out onto the stage, turned to look at the audience—and when I saw all of those faces looking up at me, watching me, waiting for me to do something, I was struck with panic. I stared openmouthed at the audience until my teacher whispered my lines to me from backstage. Then in a shaky voice I said, "There's gold in America. We'll rike it stritch in the new land!"

Everyone laughed. My parents got the whole thing on videotape. They still laugh when they watch it.

And that's exactly how I feel when I'm around girls. I might as well be in front of an audience, openmouthed, and messing up my lines.

I glanced over at Tony. He was leaning back in his chair in a casual sort of way. I wondered if he'd invented a cool way of sitting just like he'd invented a cool way of walking. By the time we reached the end of the year he'd probably have all of the glitches worked out of his routines. By the time we reached high school, he'd have reached such heights of coolness that girls would trail him around the hallways at school just to experience the cool breeze flowing from his body.

And I'd be in a corner somewhere saying everything backward.

Maybe Tony was right. Maybe it was time to invent a cool McKay. I leaned back in my chair like Tony and tried to look like I was unconcerned about math class. I thought cool thoughts. Holding my pencil loosely in my hands, I tapped it against my notebook like I was playing the drums. I glanced over at Serena to see if she'd noticed the new me. She was staring straight ahead. I wondered how long it would take girls to notice me once I became cool.

Mrs. Swenson handed out a worksheet for us to do, and I put it on top of my notebook and continued to play the drums with it. What did cool people do when they didn't know how to do a worksheet? I thought about this for a moment, then thought about playing the drums, and whether or not there were any professional ballplayers who also played in a band. That would be the ultimate cool thing to do.

I was thinking about this, and not about where I was tapping my pencil, when I missed my notebook and hit the metal edging on my desk. There was a loud twang, and half the classroom looked over at me to see what I was doing. I slumped down in my chair.

Mrs. Swenson got that dour expression on her face. "Are you finished with your worksheet already, McKay? Because if you are, perhaps you'd like to work some of the equations on the board for the rest of the class to see."

"Uh, no." I gulped. "I'm not done yet. I was just figuring them out." I slumped even lower in my chair.

I don't know why I looked over at Serena right then. Something just made me. I glanced over at her, and sure enough, she was looking back at me. Watching. Waiting for me to do something.

I bent over the worksheet and under my breath, said, "We'll rike it stritch in the new land."

At home I continued to be a model son in order to persuade my parents I did, indeed, need a room of my own. That night after dinner while I cleared off the table and Mom put things in the dishwasher, I asked her, "Did you and Dad talk about moving Kirk out of my room?"

"Well, we talked about moving you into the office."

"Me?" I dropped the last of the silverware into the sink. "Why do I have to be the one to move?"

"Because you're the one who wants his own room."

"But Kirk's the one that's impossible to live with."

Mom handed me a dishcloth and pointed at the table. It was my job to wash it off, but Mom always had to remind me to do it. "Kirk's been in that room since he was a baby. It's the only room he's ever known. It will be easier on him to be alone if he's still in familiar surroundings."

"But all the stuff in that room is mine. It's decorated with posters of my favorite baseball players."

"They're Kirk's favorite players too," Mom said. But she knew as well as I did that the only reason Kirk liked baseball was because I'd taught him about it. He probably didn't care about the players at all. If I had told him all about congressmen, he'd be just as happy with posters of U.S. senators hanging on the walls.

"I know it's not exactly fair," Mom said, "but neither is me lugging my entire office into my bedroom. If you want your own room, you'll have to make some concessions."

I knew the kind of concessions she was talking about were not the kind that sold hot dogs at baseball games. She meant I had to let Kirk have his own way before he even asked for it. It seemed like Kirk always got his own way.

"But don't you think Kirk would like to decorate a room with something he likes?" I asked. "Something with cowboys or astronauts or trains?"

Mom poured the dish soap into its tray and snapped the lid shut. "Kirk does like trains," she said. "Maybe he'd like that even better than staying in your room with the baseball players." She straightened up, then surveyed the table to make sure I'd done a good enough job with it. It must have passed her review, because she took the dishcloth instead of handing it back to me. As she wiped off the counters, she called, "Kirk!" A few moments later he trotted in.

Mom put on the overly happy face she always uses to try to get Kirk excited about something. "Hey, sweetheart, I was just thinking about how much you like trains, and I thought maybe you'd like to spend more time with some trains."

"Are we going someplace?" Kirk asked hopefully.

"Well, no. I was just thinking maybe we could decorate the office with train things. Would you like that?"

"Yeah," Kirk said slowly, as though he knew there was a catch but wasn't sure where.

"Maybe you could even pretend it was your own private train compartment on a real train."

"Yeah," Kirk said with more enthusiasm. "And I could take suitcases."

"And then wouldn't it be fun to move your bed in with all of the train things?"

"No!" His face scrunched up, and he put his hands on his hips. "I'm not moving to the office. I want to sleep in my baseball room." He stomped off, hands still on his hips, and Mom didn't call him back.

She sighed and wiped the counters for a minute longer. "We'll give him a little time to adjust to the idea."

I figured he could adjust while I moved his things out, but I didn't say so. I was being a model child.

Still, later that night as I lay in bed, I stared at the ceiling and wondered whether I'd be like my dad and have to share my room until I left home. Then I thought about my dad's job, and ROs, and how much extra money my parents would need to buy a bigger house.

Were there really secrets to selling things, like Tony had said? Would they work on selling anything? And if so, could Tony's dad teach them to my dad?

I didn't imagine my dad would want to go over to the Manetti's house for salesman lessons, but maybe Tony's dad could tell me the secrets. Then I'd show my dad how easy it was to sell things, and he'd change his mind about being a salesman. Maybe he'd become really good at it. Then we wouldn't have to worry about money anymore, and my parents would never again argue about the credit card bills, or where we went on vacation, or whether it was okay to buy juice boxes for our school lunches. Maybe someday we'd even own a BMW like the Manettis.

All I needed to do was learn the secrets.

The next day before I went to school, I searched through the filing cabinet where Dad kept his paperwork for his job. After a few minutes I found a brochure on Hendricks reverse osmosis systems. It didn't look very interesting. Mostly it was stuff about filters and workmanship. Still, I shoved it in my backpack to study later. Before I finished shoving, I noticed the price for the system. Six hundred and ninety-nine dollars.

I almost gave up any idea of salesmanship right then.

Six hundred and ninety-nine dollars? For something that just gave you water? Who'd buy that?

But I knew the answer. Tons of people. You only had to take one taste of the tap water to convince yourself you wanted to get your drinking water from somewhere else. So you could either buy a reverse osmosis system that filtered out whatever it was that caused the bad taste, or buy bottled water. You could even order water and have it brought to your door straight from—the TV advertising promised—some crystal-clear and pristine spring that looked like the fountain of youth. Or you could do what my parents did: take water jugs to the grocery store and fill them up at 25 cents a gallon at the water machine.

Six hundred and ninety-nine dollars.

At 25 cents a gallon you could buy . . . I took a moment to do the math . . . 2,796 gallons of water for $699.

How long would it take for a reverse osmosis system to pay for itself?

I didn't try to figure it out. It seemed too much like an algebra problem.

Dang. Mrs. Swenson had told us all along that we'd use algebra in real life. Maybe she was right after all.

I swung my backpack up over my shoulder and headed for

the front door. The price of the RO didn't matter. After all, Tony's dad sold houses. They were a lot more expensive than RO systems. If he could sell a house, he could tell me how to sell a water purifier.

After school, while Tony's dad drove us to the ballpark, I decided to bring up the subject. Instead of goofing off in the backseat with Tony, I leaned toward the driver's seat and said, "Coach Manetti, you're good at selling houses, right?"

"I'd like to think so," he said.

"What are the secrets?"

"The secrets?"

"Yeah, you know, the secrets to selling stuff."

He shrugged. "Well, in general, I guess I'd have to say you get a good product and then show the buyer how the product will improve his life. And if the buyer doesn't bite the first time around, you keep working on it until you find something he does want. You be persistent."

I took the brochure out of my backpack and unfolded it. "So, if I were going to sell a reverse osmosis system to you, I'd have to tell you about its twelve-month warranty and how much better off you'd be drinking fresh, clean water straight from a Hendricks system."

"Right," Coach Manetti said.

"It has four filters that completely take out color, odor, and bad taste. It also takes out microorganisms. You wouldn't want to drink those, would you?"

"I guess not," he said.

I waited a moment. "So, do you want to buy a Hendricks RO from my dad?"

The coach glanced back at me for a moment. "You're really trying to sell me one?"

"Sure. Is this the part where I get persistent?"

Coach Manetti shook his head and laughed. "I walked right into that one, didn't I?"

"Microorganisms could probably kill you," I said.

Coach Manetti looked at me through the rearview mirror. "When did your dad start selling ROs?"

"He just started. Do you want to see a brochure? It costs six hundred and ninety-nine dollars, but it'll pay for itself. Sometime." I dropped the brochure on the seat beside him. "How long do I have to be persistent for? Hours? Days?"

He laughed again and said, "Okay, okay. I guess I have been thinking about getting an RO. I'll call your dad when I run out of my supply of bottled water."

I leaned back into my seat and smiled. Not only did I now know the secrets, but I'd made a sale on my first attempt. It was easy. My dad would be so impressed. He'd be grateful, he'd be a great salesman—maybe he'd even get a promotion or something, and a new house with a nice big empty room for me couldn't be far away.

Tony rolled his eyes at me, and I knew he thought my salesman's routine was silly, but he could afford to think that. Tony had always had his own room.

We got to the baseball field and did our normal warm-ups. While we were waiting to bat, Tony and I sat next to each other on the bench. He stretched out his legs and leaned back as much as he could without falling off of the bench altogether.

"I talked to Rachel today." He said this in a louder-than-normal voice, so I knew that part of the reason he was telling me was to impress the other guys on the bench.

"Oh? Were you funny, honest, attractive, loyal, and understanding?"

"Definitely." He surveyed the field and nodded slightly. "I think she likes me. I told her I played ball, and she ought to come and watch one of the games sometime." Now he looked over at me with half a smile. "She said she'd bring Serena with her."

I felt both dread and excitement. It was flattering to think Serena might come to one of the games. I liked the idea of her sitting in the bleachers rooting for me, watching me do something I did well. The next Monday at school she would look at me admiringly and say, "I never knew you were such an athlete, McKay. Suddenly I find you the most interesting boy in the eighth grade."

But then there was the dread. What exactly had Tony said about me? I could just imagine his conversation with Rachel. "Yeah, McKay really likes Serena. Just today in algebra I was telling him he had to name their firstborn after me. . . ." And of course, Rachel would immediately pass on any information she got from Tony to Serena, which meant that rather than face her every day, I would have to go live in a monastery in Tibet.

I lowered my voice so the other guys wouldn't hear me. "What did you tell Rachel about me?"

Tony's smile grew. He knew he had me gripped in suspense, and he liked it. "I didn't say a whole lot to her about you, but I did tell her you thought Serena was cute."

On one hand this wasn't as bad as it could have been. Thinking someone was cute was not as bad as say, telling a girl you were already planning what to name your children. Still, it made me angry that Tony had talked to Rachel about me at all.

I stared at Tony. "Great."

Tony raised an eyebrow in surprise. "But you do think she's cute, don't you?"

"It's as good as telling Serena I like her. I might as well walk around with an I Have a Crush on Serena sign on my shirt."

"Well, don't you want to know if she likes you? Rachel said she'd ask Serena what she thought of you."

I put my hands over my face and groaned. I could almost feel my ego shrinking as we spoke. "No, I don't want to know. I've had two conversations with her, and one of them was about the letter x. I know what she thinks of me. She thinks I'm strange. I wanted to have a few more conversations with her just to prove I'm a normal person before I even asked her to help me with my homework, and now Rachel is going to tell her that I like her. Double great."

Tony got that don't-be-a-baby-McKay look on his face again. "You need help with your homework right now. If she doesn't like you, then we'll have to find someone else in our math class who does."

"No, we won't, because I've decided to pay for a tutor." After the last few days, an expensive, funny-smelling guy who spits seemed like good company. "And from now on, don't tell anyone anything about me. I don't need your help when it comes to girls."

"You need somebody's help. Unless you plan to run for the most-likely-to-wind-up-a-loser award." He shook his head, then stood up to take his turn at bat.

Usually I love baseball practice. Nothing makes me happier than seeing that little white ball soar through the sky. It makes me feel like I'm soaring too. But today everything felt heavy. Tony and I didn't say anything to each other for the rest of practice. I was so mad at him, every time I threw the ball to third I purposely aimed for his stomach. He always caught the ball, but still, he gave me dirty looks, like he knew what I was doing.

Isn't that the way life goes? I hadn't been in a fight with Tony since fifth grade, when he wouldn't believe that Baby Ruth candy bars weren't named after Babe Ruth. We'd argued about who knew more about baseball and ended up not talking to each other for a week. Three years we'd gone without fighting, and now after less than a week of trying to impress girls, we were mad at each other.

Girls just had a way of changing everything. That was a good enough reason not to get involved with them.

When I got home from practice, I took Kirk aside and sat

down on the couch with him. "Kirk," I said, putting my arm around him, "You're in kindergarten this year. You're getting to be a big guy, and as your older brother I have some words of wisdom for you. Some day one of the girls in your class will want to hold your hand. Take my advice. Just don't do it."

It wasn't until I was getting ready for bed that I remembered to tell Dad about my first sale. Then, with toothbrush in hand and wearing my pajamas, I went and found him in the family room. He was relaxing on the couch with the newspaper and didn't pay any attention to me as I walked in.

I sat down on the couch by him. "Hey Dad, Coach Manetti says he'll buy an RO from you."

Dad glanced at me, then looked back at the paper. "Why would he do that?"

"Because I talked to him about it. He told me the secrets to selling things, and then I turned around and used them on him."

Dad chuckled. "And so now he's buying an RO?"

"Yep."

"That's great. Next time see if he'll buy a bridge or two."

"No, I'm serious. Coach Manetti wants to buy an RO from you."

Dad held his paper down a little and looked at me. "Did he give you any money?"

"Well, no."

"Then I think the coach was pulling your leg."

◇

"No, he's just waiting until he uses up his bottled water, and then he's going to call you to buy one."

Dad chuckled again. "It seems like he sold you a bill of goods, not the other way around."

"He's really going to call you," I said, and walked out of the family room.

Okay, granted, maybe it's hard to take a business transaction seriously when the person who tells you about it is wearing pajamas and carrying a toothbrush, but still Dad ought to have realized I would have known if Coach Manetti was pulling my leg. The coach said he'd call my dad, and he would. I knew he would. After all, the Manettis had money. What was an RO system to them? He'd call, and then Dad would see I was right. Maybe he'd even start listening to me when I told him something.

*T*he next day was Saturday, and we had a game against the East Mesa Firebrands. I wondered how Tony would act toward me. The truth was that while I didn't want to fight with him anymore, I didn't exactly want to apologize to him either. What would I say I was sorry for? I just wanted to forget yesterday ever happened.

When I got to the ball field, Tony walked over to me and nodded toward the bleachers. "Adam the Magnificent, Mr. Baseball himself, is here to watch us play."

I looked up and saw Jenna with a tall blond guy.

"Jenna is paying me five dollars not to blow her cover," he said, "but that doesn't mean *you* can't talk to them."

I smiled back at Tony because he obviously wanted to forget yesterday too. "Should I ask her who her favorite shortstop is?"

He smirked. "She'd probably say Mark McGwire. Whenever she doesn't know what to say she just talks about him."

Then Coach Manetti called us over to do our warm-ups, and

I didn't think about Jenna and Adam until the game ended. We played a good game and won by four runs, but even so Adam came over to give us a critique of our baseball skills.

While Tony and I were putting equipment in the back of the Manetti's Silverado, Jenna and Adam sauntered up next to us. Adam patted Tony on the shoulder. "Hey, that was a nice scoop of the line drive—but you could have made the double play if you'd fired off to second instead of settling for the sure out."

"Uh, right," Tony said.

"And you could have shown a little more hustle too."

Tony forced a smile. "I'll try to keep that in mind for next time."

Adam turned and looked at me. "But hey, McKay, good hit in the second."

Jenna nodded. "Yeah, the way you hit reminded me of Mark McGwire."

"How about the way I batted?" Tony asked.

"You were more like Randy Johnson," she said.

Jenna may not have realized Randy Johnson was a pitcher and a lousy batter, but Tony glared at her anyway. Adam, however, laughed heartily and patted Tony on the shoulder. "Oh, I wouldn't say you were *that* bad."

"Thanks," Tony said. "Thanks a lot."

"Of course that stance of yours could use some work," Adam said.

Jenna nodded at Adam in agreement. "I tell him that all the time."

"Hey, Jenna," Tony said slowly. "Who's your favorite short-stop?"

Jenna smiled in a strained sort of way. "You are, of course."

"I'm not a shortstop. I play third base."

"True, but you're still shorter than I am, and I'm always telling you to stop."

Tony said, "Uh-huh," and I could tell he was deciding how badly he wanted that five dollars.

I guess Jenna could tell too because she reached over and took Adam's hand. "Do you want to go and get something to eat now?"

"Sure," he said, and then to us, "See you guys later."

As they walked off, we could hear Jenna say, "Thanks for watching my little brother play and giving him tips on how to play better and everything. I know the kids really appreciate help from a pro."

I elbowed Tony and whispered, "Oh, yeah. We really appreciate help from a pro."

"What an idiot," Tony said. "It's hard to even feel sorry for him. I hope she's so convincing that he wills his entire baseball card collection to her."

I put the bat bag into the truck then turned and watched Jenna get into Adam's car.

"Hey, Tony, do you think a girl will ever pretend to like baseball to impress us?"

"We can always hope."

"Naw, I wouldn't like that. When I start dating, I'll want to know what a girl's really like, not just what she's pretending to be like."

Tony just shrugged, so I pressed the point. "I mean, how would you feel if you thought you knew a girl, and then found out everything you thought about her was a lie?"

"I don't know," he said. "How cute is this girl we're talking about?"

I tossed the bases into the truck and then shut the tailgate. "I don't know why I even asked you. You're the guy who's going to fake being honest so girls will think he's Mr. Right."

"And it's working, too. I called Rachel last night, and she was completely interested when I told her all about the Boy Scouts law." He held up his fingers into the Boy Scouts sign. "A scout is trustworthy, loyal, helpful, friendly, courteous, kind, obedient, cheerful, thrifty, brave, clean, and reverent. I've got loyalty plus all that other stuff down pat."

"Of course," I said. "Why didn't I see it before? The whole purpose of the scouting program is to turn you into someone a girl would like."

"On Monday I'm going to be funny and attractive."

"Try being brilliant, fascinating, and humble while you're at it."

We walked away from the truck and toward the bleachers, where a lot of the parents were still talking to each other. Tony grinned over at me. "Just watch, on Monday I'm going to be such a Mr. Right that pretty soon people will think there were three Wright brothers—Orville, Wilbur, and Tony."

"Yeah, yeah. Don't try to leave the ground just yet."

My parents had been talking with some of the other parents. Now they came over and asked if I was ready to go. I told Tony I'd see him later and walked with my parents to our car. All the way there I thought about Tony's plans and wondered if they'd work. Maybe he'd fool everyone, just like Jenna was fooling Adam, and he'd become wildly popular. But no matter how I turned it around in my mind, I still didn't like it. I knew I could never be all phony just to get a girl to like me.

On Sunday I told Kirk over and over again how neat his new room would be. It didn't matter. Kirk refused to adjust. It didn't matter that I'd bribed him with decorations of trains, dinosaurs, or his own baseball players. I could have promised him the whole cast of *Barney and Friends* to sing him to sleep every night, and he still wouldn't have wanted to move. He wanted *his* closet, *his* window, and *his* posters, which unfortunately also happened to be *my* closet, *my* window, and *my* posters.

I guess I could have given in and volunteered to move, but it just seemed so unfair. After all, it had been my room first. I had picked out the baseball border that matched the curtains, which matched my bedspread. I had bought those posters of Cal Ripkin, Mark McGwire, and Sammy Sosa with my own money. And besides, the office was smaller. Since Kirk was a smaller person, with smaller stuff, he should have the smaller room.

Mom and Dad said they'd try to reason with Kirk about it.

Since when has reason solved anything in the world? Look at the United Nations. They've been trying to work problems out with reason for decades, and we're no closer to world peace than we ever were.

That night I tried my own methods to convince Kirk to move.

"Kirk," I said as we got ready for bed, "I haven't told you this before, but there's buried treasure somewhere in the office."

Kirk pulled on his pajama bottoms and surveyed me skeptically. "What kind of treasure?"

"Gold and silver," I whispered in awed tones, but when he didn't look impressed with this treasure, I added, "And Hot Wheels, and flashlights, and swords. If you move into the office, I bet you'll be able to find it."

Kirk's eyes had grown wide when I'd mentioned the Hot Wheels, flashlights, and swords, but then narrowed when I'd mentioned moving.

"How come Mom and Dad have never told me about the treasure?"

"They don't know about it. It was left there by the people who owned the house before we did. They were pirates." Actually, they were retired schoolteachers, but that's the beauty of being the oldest. Kirk wasn't around, so he couldn't argue the point. I continued slowly, "I discovered a map for the treasure. I was going to find it myself, but if you agree to move to the office, I'll give you the map."

Kirk pulled on the top to his pajamas carefully. I knew he was thinking it over.

"And I'll tell you another secret." I looked under the bed quickly as I said this. "I've also discovered a bunch of monsters have moved into this room. I think I'd better stay here and fight them off so they don't eat anyone."

Kirk put his hands on his hips. "Uh-uuuhh."

"Yes-huh." I flung the closet door open quickly and jabbed my hand into the clothes a few times. "And they're the kind of monsters that eat five-year-old boys."

With his hands still on his hips, Kirk said, "You're just trying to scare me so I'll move out."

I put my arm against the back wall of the closet and acted like I was being sucked in. "Oh, no!" I yelled. "One's got me now!"

Kirk let out a scream and ran down the hallway to our parents' room. Which just goes to show you, if I ever was attacked by something, Kirk wouldn't help me, so I shouldn't feel bad about occasionally teasing him.

After a few minutes, Dad came into the room holding Kirk's hand and gave me a stern lecture about putting ideas into my brother's head. I don't know what Dad was worried about. If I could really put ideas in Kirk's head, somewhere along the line the idea that he should move into the office would have stuck. But no dice. Kirk is more stubborn than all the United Nations put together.

On Monday morning Tony showed up at my locker with a list scribbled on his notebook. "I think Mr. Right needs an exciting hobby to make him more attractive. Which do you think sounds better—mountain climbing or scuba diving?"

"How about wrestling wild animals with your bare hands?"

"Yeah, that would be cool. Too bad I don't have any big scars." While we waited for school to start, we walked toward the library, and Tony kept looking at his notebook. "Maybe I should pretend I've done both. That would make me twice as attractive, right?"

I shifted my books from one hand to the other. "You're not really going to tell people you've been mountain climbing and scuba diving, are you?"

"I hike. I swim. It's technically not even a lie. Besides I researched both sports on the Internet last night, so I'll know what I'm talking about."

We walked through the library doors and saw Serena, Rachel, and their friend Anna sitting at one of the tables. Brian Vanders was also there. He was a linebacker on the football team and a decent player at that, but I bet he couldn't hit a home run to save his life. Still, all the girls sat listening to him talk, and from the looks on their faces it seemed he was doing a pretty good Mr. Right impersonation himself.

Tony was not daunted. Using his cool walk, he strolled up to the table and sat down. I followed, but not quite as smoothly. When I pulled my chair back, I rammed it into my shin. I sat down anyway and tried not to wince. I wondered if Serena had seen me do this and whether girls ever thought that guys who rammed chairs into their legs could be Mr. Right.

"Hi, guys," Tony said.

Everyone returned his greeting except for Brian. He just scowled in a smiling sort of way.

"We've been talking about concerts," Rachel told us. "Do your parents let you go?"

"Maybe if it were a Pavarotti concert," I said. The girls all looked at me blankly, so I said, "My parents don't like rock music. They listen to classical."

Anna wrinkled her nose. "You don't get to listen to rock?" Apparently this was a Mr. Wrong thing to do.

"I listen to it sometimes," I said. I liked country better, but I wasn't about to say anything else until I was sure it wouldn't cause any more nose wrinkling.

Tony said, "My parents don't worry about me at concerts. They're more worried about the other stuff I do, like mountain climbing."

Brian looked skeptical. "You've been mountain climbing? Where?"

Tony glanced at his notebook. "Oh, lots of places. Like Mount McKinley."

Serena's eyes widened. "Wow, you've been to Alaska?"

Tony glanced at his notebook again. "Yes I have, because that's where Mount McKinley is."

"When did you go there?" Rachel asked.

"A couple of summers ago. My uncle took me. He's really into climbing."

I said, "You're talking about your uncle Orville, right?"

"Right," Tony said.

"Weren't you really cold?" Anna asked.

"Sure, but it was worth it. Besides we had on really thick coats and boots, and a lot of other technical mountain-climbing stuff you've probably never heard of before."

"Did you take many pictures?" Serena asked.

"Tons," Tony said. "I was so mad when that bear ate my camera and ruined them all."

Rachel gasped. "A bear ate your camera?"

Tony nodded solemnly. "You run into a lot of wild animals in the mountains."

"How scary," Anna said.

"How exciting," Serena added.

"How far did you get up the mountain?" Brian asked.

Tony hesitated. I could tell he hadn't researched this question. Finally he said, "Farther than most people get."

Brian leaned back in his chair and gave a casual shrug. "Why do it the hard way? If you want to see the top of the mountain, why not just do what I'm going to do? Fly."

Tony raised an eyebrow. "Oh, you're sprouting wings soon?"

"No, my dad has his own plane, a Beechcraft Bonanza. He's been giving me lessons. When I turn sixteen, I'll get to fly solo."

All three girls cooed and then asked him things all at once. "What's the plane like?" "How hard is it to learn to fly?" "Where are you going to go?"

Brian happily answered all of their questions until the bell rang. Then, when everyone got up to go, he walked next to Serena out of the library. He smiled over at her. "Who knows," he said, "maybe after I get my pilot's license, I'll be able to take someone up with me."

She looked back at him admiringly. "That would be really neat."

"Remember to bring a parachute," I said, but only Tony heard me.

The two of us headed down a different hallway than the others, but none of them told us good-bye.

As we walked, Tony shuffled his feet. "Dang. I knew I should have gone with the scuba diving."

"It isn't fair," I said. "I bet Brian doesn't even need an algebra tutor."

Tony glanced over at me. "Brian did seem to be zeroing in on Serena, didn't he?"

I didn't answer.

"Well, you're just going to have to be cooler than he is."

"How could I possibly be cooler than flying an airplane? You weren't even cooler than Brian, and your camera was eaten by wild bears."

"Yeah."

We walked in silence for a few more moments, and then Tony resumed his foot-shuffling. "I'll tell you one thing. When I do tell the scuba-diving story, there are going to be sharks in it, and lots of them."

*   *   *

I figured that after being outperformed in the library, Tony would give his Mr. Right routine a rest. But at lunchtime when he sat down beside me, he leaned over and grinned. "Guess who I just talked to?"

"The chairman of the scuba diving club?"

"Rachel." He gave me a grin, then said, "Don't you think she's one of the cutest girls in our class?"

"Sure." I hadn't actually made a list or anything, but I suppose if I had, Rachel would have been on it.

"Did you ever notice that she wears eyeshadow?"

I ripped open my packet of potato chips and popped a few into my mouth. "No, I've never paid that much attention to Rachel's eyelids."

"Well, neither have I, but she said she just bought some new makeup yesterday. Get this: She has four shades of eyeshadow, and they're all brown. Does that seem weird, or what?"

"It seems weird that you were talking about eyeshadow with her."

"We talked about other things too. She loved the shark stories." He looked thoughtful for a moment. "I think she really likes me, because, you know, she always laughs at my jokes. You can tell if a girl likes you by how much she laughs at your jokes. Rachel even laughs when I say stupid stuff."

I wasn't sure this was the best compliment you could give a girl, but I didn't say anything. Tony was clearly the girl expert, so who was I to question his methods of judging them? I listened to him go on about Rachel, and he acted as though they'd been close for years instead of just on talking terms for the last few days.

"Oh, and I got an answer back from Serena too." Tony took a long sip from his juice box to draw out the suspense. "She said that Serena said she thinks you're kinda cute."

"Kinda cute? That sounds like the way you'd describe a gerbil or something. 'Kinda cute' probably means she didn't want to hurt my feelings."

"Give yourself a break," Tony said. "She likes you."

"Oh." I still didn't believe him. I wondered if she'd ever describe Brian as being "kinda cute."

"So go find her and ask her if she'll help you with algebra."

"You know, maybe I don't need a tutor. Maybe if I agreed to wash Mrs. Swenson's car every day, she'd give me extra credit."

Tony gave me a blank stare.

"Or maybe if I just shut myself in a room and pressed the book to my forehead, the knowledge would seep out into my brain."

"Or maybe a little man named Rumpelstiltskin will appear and offer to do your homework in exchange for your firstborn child."

"I'd take it under consideration."

"Ask Serena to help you with your algebra today," Tony said. "*Today.*"

I sighed, and it was a deep and resigned sigh. "Okay. I'll ask her."

* * *

I only had two times left during the day that I was likely to see Serena: at PE, and wandering around the hall between classes. I tried to think of something preplanned to say to her. Something casual yet fascinating. Something that had nothing to do with the letters one did or didn't use in algebra equations.

During PE we went outside to play softball. This was an incredible stroke of good fortune for me because the baseball diamond was my second home. I didn't have to try and look cool with a bat in my hand. It happened naturally. It was the perfect way to impress Serena. And after she was sufficiently impressed, it would be easier to talk to her. I'd strike up a conversation about softball, she'd tell me how wonderful I was at it, then I'd say, "Yeah, but I'm lousy at algebra. I really wish someone would help me out with it. . . ."

Luck was with me again when Mr. Gibson, our PE teacher, divided us into teams. Serena and I were on the same one. I didn't manage to stand anywhere near her when we were batting—she hung in the back of the line by some other girls, and the team insisted I be the fourth batter so I could hit everyone home—but I figured I'd have a chance to talk to her in the outfield.

When it was my turn at bat, the bases were loaded and the other team's players all moved back. I love it when they do that. I hit the ball high and clear over second base. It would have been quite impressive if I had made it home, but the runner in front of me was being cautious and stopped at third. I couldn't very well run over him, so I was stuck on second. Still, it was two runs. I looked at the line of batters to see if I could tell whether Serena was impressed or not, but she was talking with Anna and didn't seem to be paying attention to the game at all.

Later, when I made it home, I went and stood at the end of the batting line. Serena and Anna had mysteriously not moved up any since we'd started the game. As I stood by them, Serena said, "You can go in front of us, McKay. We don't want to bat."

She'd spoken to me. This was my opportunity to speak back to her, only I wasn't sure what to say. "Why not?" I settled on, and immediately congratulated myself for not saying anything stupid.

"We don't like baseball," Anna told me.

"Well, you're in luck then, because this isn't baseball. It's softball." Personally, I didn't think this was a stupid thing to say, but Anna gave me a look that indicated she disagreed.

"Same thing," she said.

"Oh, come on, this is tons of fun. I mean, how many other times in life do you get to hit something with a bat?" Talking to Serena was not nearly as hard as I thought it would be. This was actually going well. I could practically picture myself telling Tony all about it. I'd sort of toss my head around like he always did, and then in the same casual tone he used, I'd say, "Yeah, I talked to Serena during PE today. . . ."

Serena shrugged some of her long brown hair off one shoulder. "I never hit anything at all. I always strike out. I'd rather just stay at the back of the line and hope Mr. Gibson doesn't notice me." She peered over at the field to where our PE teacher was pitching the balls. "Is he looking over here?"

"I don't think so."

"Could you sort of stand in front of us, just in case?" This is probably not the type of attention girls give to Sammy Sosa or Ken Griffey Jr., but at this point I was willing to take anything, so I stood in front of Serena and Anna while we continued to discuss the merits of baseball.

Me: It's the all-American pastime.
Them: But it's so hot out in the sun.
Me: It's the greatest game ever invented.
Them (whining): And besides, we hate chasing after the balls.

We talked some more about athletics, specifically how Serena and Anna didn't like to play or watch any sporting events. What do girls do in their spare time, anyway?

Our team got its third out, so we headed onto the field. As we walked, Serena said, "McKay, do you want to still stand in front of us? That way, if any balls come our way, you'll be able to get them."

"I'm on second," I told her. "But if you stand behind me, I'll see what I can do."

So Serena and Anna went and stood about forty feet past

second base and tried to continue chatting without letting the game get in their way. And I was as good as my word. The few times a ball was hit in their direction, I backed up into the outfield and got it. Once I even caught the ball to make our second out. All runners had been wavering between bases while the ball was in the air, and then had to make quick backtracks after I made the catch. I fired off the ball to third and nearly got the runner out there too. It was a spectacular play, and I'm sure Serena would have been impressed enough to help me with algebra equations right there on the spot had she been paying any attention. Unfortunately she was speaking with Anna and seemed only vaguely aware we were playing softball at all.

This should have been my first clue that I needed to be careful when I ran around retrieving balls. I should have paid more attention to where Serena was standing. I shouldn't have just expected she'd move out of my way.

When the next ball flew over second base, I saw my chance to make the third out and impress everyone with my athletic skill yet another time. The ball was higher than I'd have liked, and I knew I'd have to sprint to catch it. I took off running into the outfield, all of the time keeping my eye on the ball. That's when the crash happened. I'm not sure which part of Serena I ran over first, only that suddenly I was on the ground in a tangled heap with Serena at the bottom.

At first I was so surprised I didn't say anything at all, then I pulled myself up and said, "Are you okay?"

She said something like, "Uheergh," which didn't sound like a good answer.

Anna came and leaned over her. "Can you get up?"

"I think so," she said, but she only sat up.

"I'm so sorry," I told Serena. "I . . . I didn't see you."

About a dozen people, including Mr. Gibson, ran over to us. "Are you hurt?" he asked her.

"Just my knee." Her face looked white, and she winced as she tried to straighten her leg out.

Mr. Gibson knelt down in front of her and examined her knee. "Where does it hurt?"

Serena bit her lip, and I could tell she was trying not to cry. "Everywhere."

"We'd better get you to the health office and get some ice on it." Mr. Gibson stood up and then helped Serena to her feet. "Do you think you can walk if someone helps you?"

She nodded, but she didn't look confident.

Anna said, "I'll help you," and then half a dozen girls chimed in that they'd help too. They moved off the field in a great mass of sympathy.

Mr. Gibson blew his whistle and said, "All right, the rest of you get back to the game," then followed after the girls.

I slapped little pieces of dirt and grass off of my pants and walked back to second base. I didn't pay much attention to the game after that. Even after Serena and her friends had gone into the school, somehow I still saw her in my mind hobbling across

◇

the grass toward the building. Everything had happened so fast, I barely had enough time to tell her I was sorry, and she hadn't said anything to me at all. She hadn't said anything, but I could be fairly certain she wasn't impressed with my athletic skill.

I took a long, deep sigh. It had been eight years since the holding-hands incident with Stephanie Morris in kindergarten. Eight years since I tried to get a girl to like me. And after today, it just might take me another eight years to make my next try.

*T*hat night after dinner while I cleared off the table and Mom put things in the dishwasher, I told her she needed to find me a tutor for algebra.

"Really?" She looked surprised I had brought it up. "Your math class still isn't going well even after you've been doing your homework every day?"

"I do it, but I get it all wrong. I'm too far behind to understand it on my own."

Mom rinsed off a plate, then put it into a slot in the dishwasher. "Well, McKay, I think it's very responsible of you to realize when you need help and to ask for it. I'll call the school and see if they can recommend someone." She smiled a bit. "And because I can see you really are trying to do better, maybe your father and I will help pay for the cost."

I put a handful of plates into the sink. "Thanks." It was the best news I'd had all day.

My jobs were finished, but I still stayed in the kitchen while Mom put the rest of the plates in the dishwasher and filled the soap dispenser. Mom was so mommish. It was hard to believe she'd ever been a teenager.

"Mom, did you ever, you know, *like* anybody when you were my age?"

She shrugged. "I suppose I was interested in a couple of guys."

"Would you still have been interested in them if they'd crashed into you during PE and hurt your knee?"

Mom shut the dishwasher and looked over at me. "McKay, did you run into someone in PE?"

I nodded.

"Was she okay?"

"I don't know. She went to the health office. But I have a feeling she won't think I'm kinda cute anymore."

Mom said, "Oh," in a sad sort of way and then, "Did you tell her you were sorry?"

I nodded again.

"Maybe you could send her a card or something."

Kirk walked over to where I stood. I hadn't even known he was around, or I wouldn't have told Mom about Serena at all. That's the beauty of only being five years old. You're so short people overlook you, and you get to hear their conversations. With a serious expression on his face he asked, "Did you kill someone?"

"No," I told him. "Not this time."

He seemed a little disappointed. "Was there lots of blood?"

"Nope. None at all."

"Well, I'd send her flowers anyway." Kirk then broke out into a commercial jingle tune. "Say it with flowers and lighter her day. She'll know you're lumpy in every way."

It's supposed to be: Say it with flowers and light up her day. She'll know you love her in every way. I didn't correct him.

Mom picked up the dishrag and wiped off the edges of the sink. "I think McKay is a little young to be sending girls flowers."

"The girl on the TV liked it," Kirk said. "She wrapped her arms around the guy's neck like she was going to squeeze his head right off."

"You watch too much TV," Mom said.

"I bet nobody could squeeze McKay's head off." Kirk tilted his face sideways and gave me a studious look as though he was trying to determine how sturdy my head was.

I left to go do my homework before Kirk could start requesting neck-squeezing demonstrations.

I tried to keep my mind on the Revolutionary War, but my mind kept drifting back to Serena and flowers.

I'd never been one to take advice from my little brother, but it wasn't a bad idea. Girls did like flowers. And if I gave some to Serena, then maybe she wouldn't be mad at me and tell all of her friends at school what a jerk I was. Maybe I should get her flowers. Or maybe not. Maybe it would be a geeky thing to do.

The next day Serena wasn't at school, and Rachel told Tony, who told me, that Serena had sprained her knee and would have to stay off it for at least a week and then be on crutches for a while after that. This made me feel even worse. Serena was crippled, and it was all my fault. I had to do something for her, and Kirk's suggestion seemed like the best idea. The only problem was, there wasn't a florist store within bike riding distance.

I suppose I could have asked my mother to drive me somewhere, but she'd already said I was too young to send a girl flowers. I was afraid if I brought the subject up again, she'd get all weird about it. She'd ask me a thousand questions about Serena and give me lectures about how I shouldn't get seriously involved with girls and maybe insist on meeting Serena's parents or something. I didn't want that. No, some things were just better for a guy to do on his own. I'd have to find the flowers myself.

After I got home from school, I surveyed our backyard. We had plenty of blooming bushes and plants growing there, although they weren't really the kind of flowers you made into a bouquet.

But what other choice did I have? I could have called Tony, but he had the same type of plants in his yard. We all did. Since we live in a desert climate, there aren't many types of plants that can survive the summer, when the temperature stays above 110 for months on end.

So I could choose bright pink flowers from the prickly green bushes in the corner—although those would be hard to pick— or white flowers from the bushes by the house—which come to think of it, were poisonous. Although I knew girls didn't actually eat bouquets, still, it somehow seemed wrong to give someone a poisonous one. That left the low-growing ground-cover called lantana. It had bunches of tiny blossoms that grew together in clumps so that they looked like little purple popcorn balls. Not exactly the type of flower you see a lot of in floral arrangements.

I looked at the plants again, sighed, and decided a card would be a better choice.

Mom had a bunch of blank cards we used for different occasions, so I pulled one of those out of her desk and sat down at the table with it. I looked at the inside of the card for a few minutes, then wrote, "Dear Serena." I tried to think of something to write after that, but just tapped my pen against the card instead.

What did you write to someone you'd crashed into? "Dear Serena, I'm glad to hear nothing is broken"? "Dear Serena, I hope you don't hate me now"? Cards are so personal. That's the nice thing about flowers. You don't have to say a lot when you give someone flowers. You just hand them over, and the person says, "How nice, let me put these in water." That's it. Much easier.

I looked out at the bushes in the backyard again. Flowers are flowers. What did it matter that we didn't have the same kind you bought at the store? Besides, I'd always thought the lantana were pretty. Why wouldn't Serena like them?

I put the card in its envelope and shoved it into my back pocket. Then I checked Serena's address from the phone book and yelled to Mom that I was going for a bike ride. I went out the door to the garage, but before I got my bike, I took the side door into the backyard. We had so much lantana growing by the side of the house, I knew my parents would never notice if I took some.

I broke off stems until I had a big handful of them, then held them up and viewed them appraisingly. After a moment I held them to my face and sniffed them. They smelled faintly like dirty laundry, as though they were trying to repel the bees instead of attract them, but still they looked soft and pretty— like something a girl might like. Nice.

Of course by the time I'd peddled over to Serena's house some lantana blossoms had shaken loose, and a few of the stems were mangled, but they still looked all right.

As I walked up to Serena's door, I noticed they also had different-colored lantana in their front yard. I hoped she wouldn't think I'd picked her own flowers to give to her. It was just one reason—and suddenly I could think of many—to turn around, get back on my bike, and go home. But what if Serena had seen me already? What if she were at this moment looking out her window and happened to notice McKay standing on her driveway with a handful of flowers? Wouldn't it seem even more ridiculous to turn around now? Maybe she'd think I had come by, picked her flowers, and was about to take them somewhere else.

I took a deep breath, walked up to her door, and rang the bell. After a few moments Mrs. Kimball opened the door. She looked at me, looked at the flowers in my hand, and then looked back at me questioningly.

"I didn't pick them from your yard," I blurted out. "I got them from my house."

She still looked at me questioningly.

"They're for Serena," I said. "I came by to see how she was because I sort of plowed over her in PE yesterday."

"Oh!" Mrs. Kimball drew the word out for a few seconds. "Well, come inside." She stepped aside so I could get by. "I'm sure Serena would love to visit with you."

I followed Mrs. Kimball into their family room, where Serena was laying on the couch. She wore an old T-shirt and shorts, and her hair was kind of messy, like she hadn't combed it yet today. Her knee was wrapped in an Ace bandage and propped up on four pillows. She was gazing at the TV and looked bored.

Her mother said, "Serena, someone's here to see you."

Serena turned, saw me, and stared for a moment. "McKay, what are you doing here?" She ran her hand over her hair and shot her mother an angry look, but I wasn't sure whether she was angry at her mother for letting me in when she didn't look her best, or for just letting me in at all.

"I came by to see how you were," I said. "Oh, and to bring you these." I handed her the flowers, and a few of the lantana blossoms dropped onto her shorts. I suddenly felt silly about giving them to her, but what else could I have done? Pretend I was standing in her family room holding them for some other reason?

As she took them, she said, "Oh. Lantana. How nice."

I knew she didn't mean it. She would have used the exact same tone of voice if I'd brought her a bundle of weeds. Now she was staring at them like she didn't quite know what to do with them.

Luckily her mother came and took them from her. "I'll go put them in some water," she said. And then to me she said, "It was very sweet of you to bring them." Mrs. Kimball walked toward the kitchen with one hand holding the bouquet and the other hand underneath it to catch any more falling lantana blossoms. Over her shoulder, she called back to me, "Feel free to sit anywhere."

I sat down on a recliner close to the couch. "I'm sorry I couldn't find you better flowers. It was sort of a last-minute thing. I mean, I was just going to give you a card, but I couldn't think of what to write in it." I hadn't meant to tell her any of these things, but to prove my point, I took out the card from my pocket and gave it to her.

She opened the card and read out loud, "Dear Serena." She giggled a little and then closed the card. "You couldn't think of anything to say after that?"

"Mostly I wanted to tell you I'm sorry, but it's a big card, and 'I'm sorry' doesn't take up a lot of room."

"It's all right." She set the card down on the couch beside her. "It's not a bad sprain. The doctor said I just have to stay off it for a while."

"You're going to miss school?"

"Yeah." She said this as though she was not entirely happy about the situation. "Anna is bringing me my homework assignments." Her face brightened a bit. "You're in my math class. Maybe you could explain the stuff I miss to me."

Irony. That's what my English teacher would have called it. Here was the girl I wanted to help me in class, and she was asking me to help her.

"Uh, I'd like to," I said. "But I'm not very good in math. In fact, my mom's calling around to see about getting me a tutor."

"Really?" Serena seemed surprised. "What don't you understand?"

"All of it. I mean, I never understood how to do it in the beginning, and now I'm completely lost."

Without even seeming to think about it, she said, "I could help you with it." She waved her hand in the direction of a desk and said, "My books are over there. Bring our algebra book over."

"Now? You want to go over algebra now?"

She shrugged. "Sure. Why not? As you can see, I don't have much else to do."

And that's how my first tutoring session with Serena came to be. I would like to say that as soon as she went over the work, I completely understood how to do it, and she was stunned by my intelligence. But that's not how it happened. We went back to the beginning of the book and ground through some of the problems. It wasn't easy, but I did understand it, eventually. At least I understood the first few pages, but even that made me happy. It had been so long since I could find x

with any accuracy, I'd begun to worry that it was all beyond my comprehension. Working with Serena made me feel like there was a glimmer of hope for my passing math class.

We were just starting in on chapter three when the doorbell rang. Moments later Mrs. Kimball ushered Brian into the room. Serena looked surprised to see him, and he looked equally surprised to see me sitting beside her. He glanced from her to me in transparent annoyance.

Serena ran her hand over her hair and said, "Brian. Hi."

He walked closer to the couch. "I heard about your knee at school and thought you might need someone to help you with your social studies homework."

What he meant was: I'm here to flirt with you.

Serena smiled at him and said, "Thanks. That was really thoughtful."

What she meant was: Why do these boys keep showing up in my living room when I haven't done my hair?

He looked over at me and said, "I can explain it to you later if you're busy now."

Which meant: What is McKay doing here?

Serena glanced at me and said, "That's okay. McKay and I were just working on algebra, but we're ready to take a break now."

Which meant—well, I wasn't exactly sure, but I was afraid it meant: Sit down, Brian, I'd rather flirt with you than talk to McKay. You're much cooler, and besides, you've never plowed over me in PE class.

I said, "Actually, I ought to be going. Thanks for the help with algebra, though." I stood up, looked around for my belongings, then realized I hadn't brought anything but the flowers.

"It was really nice of you to come by, McKay," Serena said. "Stop by again and tell me what's going on in algebra class."

Meaning: My mother raised me to be polite, and I must say something to you as you're leaving.

I smiled at her. "Sure," I said, and then in an attempt at a joke, "Don't bother seeing me to the door."

Serena smiled. Brian did not. He sat down by Serena and opened his social studies book. I walked across the room. Right before I went into the hallway, I turned one last time to look back at Serena. She was watching Brian. He was telling her something, but from the smile on his face I didn't think it had anything to do with social studies.

The next day at school while I got books out of my locker, I told Tony that I'd gone over to Serena's house.

He turned and gave me a big grin. "Way to go!"

When I didn't say anything else he nudged me with his elbow. "Well, was she nice to you?"

I shrugged. "She's nice to everyone."

"Did you ask her to help you with math?"

"We went over the first two chapters of the book."

He gave me the thumbs-up signal. "Home run. Didn't I tell you it would work out? Didn't I?"

"Yeah, yeah," I said. "And we'll call our firstborn Tony. That is, if she doesn't want to call him Brian instead."

◇

"Brian?"

"He came over to give her the social studies homework."

"Really? Mr. Jet Engine himself stopped by?" Tony considered this for a moment, then nodded solemnly. "Well, I guess that's good news and bad news. The bad news is you're going to have to work even harder to get Serena to like you."

When he didn't say anything more, I asked, "So what's the good news?"

"He doesn't like Rachel, so I'm home free."

I shut my locker door and gave him a dirty look. "The next time you go mountain climbing, I hope the bear gets more than your camera."

"Oh, come on, you can take the guy on."

"Uh, right." I wasn't exactly sure what Tony meant by "taking him on." It sounded vaguely like I was supposed to punch him out in the school parking lot. I wasn't about to do that, but I did have my own ideas about seeing Serena again. She'd told me to come over to her house again and tell her what was going on in algebra class. I needed help with the assignments. What better way to accomplish both than to tape record the math class? It gave me an excuse to see Serena, and hopefully she'd help me out with the assignment at the same time.

I'd brought a handheld tape recorder to school for this purpose and was now carrying it around with my books.

Tony and I walked down the hallway to our first class. As though he'd just thought of it, Tony said, "I called Rachel last night and we talked for over an hour. I think I'll ask her to go

◇

out with me." He paused for a moment to say hello to some guys we'd just passed, then returned his attention to me. "Maybe it would help your chances with Serena if we all, you know, went out together and did something."

"Like what?" I said this not so much as a question, but as a protest. The fact that I had not forgotten, but apparently Tony had, was that we were only thirteen years old. Anywhere we went, we would have to walk, bike, or have our parents drive us. I was not thrilled about any of these three options. I mean, how impressed would a girl on crutches be if you asked her if she wanted to walk to the movies with you? Having your parents drive you would be almost as bad. It was hard enough to talk to a girl. It would be impossible to do while your parents listened in from the front seat of the family car. And I could just imagine the comments I'd get from my parents. As we got out at the movie theater, they'd say: "You didn't forget your money, did you, McKay?" or "Remember, a gentleman always holds the door open for his date," or worse yet, "Be sure you go to the bathroom before the movie starts." It would be awful. I just knew it.

Besides, my parents didn't want me to date until I was sixteen. And really, that seemed like the best time to me. At sixteen I'd have my own driver's license and a summer job. That would mean I could actually take a girl out to dinner or somewhere nice. Right now, with only my allowance money to depend on, we'd only be able to go to the nearest vending machine.

Tony shrugged his shoulders. "I don't know. I just thought it might be fun if all four of us did something together. Maybe we could go somewhere and hang out."

"Serena's knee is hurt. She can only 'hang out' on her couch."

"Oh, that's right," Tony seemed a bit disappointed. "I guess she won't be much fun for a while. Maybe I'll just ask Rachel to do something by ourselves."

Tony didn't bring up the subject again after that, and we both went to our first class. I didn't usually see him again until it was time to go to algebra class. I waited for him by my locker like I always did, but today he didn't show up. Finally I walked over to Mrs. Swenson's room by myself.

That's when I saw him outside the math class talking with Rachel. I don't know why she was there because she had English this period, and it was in a different hallway altogether—well, actually I do know why she was there. It was obvious she was there to flirt with Tony, and she was doing a good job of it. She held onto one end of a novel and Tony held onto the other.

He said, "It's my book now."

"Oh, no, it's *not*," she answered back in a syrupy teasing voice.

"Oh, yes, it *is*," he said in the same tone, and they went on this way for a few moments, fighting over who would hold the book.

When Tony looked up and saw me, he let go of the novel and said in his normal voice, "Is it time to go in already?"

I nearly said, "Oh, yes, it *is*." But instead I just said, "The bell will ring any second now."

"I guess I'd better go, or I'll be late," Rachel said. We all knew she didn't have a chance to make it to her English class on time, but she didn't seem to be bothered by this fact. She gave Tony one last wave before she turned and strolled down the hallway.

Tony grinned at me, then walked into math class. As he sauntered over to his desk, I noticed that he'd finally perfected his cool walk.

I sat down at my desk, took out my recorder, and pressed the on button. Of course, I hadn't counted on Mrs. Swenson explaining so much of today's assignment to us by doing examples on the board. I quickly realized that if the class was going to make any sense at all to Serena, she would need to know what Mrs. Swenson was doing, so I kept picking the recorder up and whispering comments into it. "Mrs. Swenson just wrote seven x over eight equals x plus three-fourths," I'd say. "Now she's miraculously found the common denominator." I felt like a sports announcer, and so I did the rest of my commentary in a sportscaster's voice. "She's stepping up to the plate," I whispered breathlessly. "Now she's moved the x to the left side of the equation. She's put those bubble things around the left side, she's moving fast now, multiply by twenty-four and divide by negative three, and she's scored! X equals negative six. The class goes wild!"

Tony passed me a note, but I was afraid if I read it, I'd miss something important, so I slipped the note into my book and kept up my description of what Mrs. Swenson was doing at the board.

When it was finally time to work on our problems, I slipped the note out and read it. It said, "Rachel and I are meeting at the mall after baseball practice. We're going to go hang out at the arcade. I'd invite you to come, but three's a crowd."

I knew he was just showing off, but I didn't care. Who wanted to be around Tony and Rachel if they were going to do stupid things like stand around and tease each other over who was going to hold some book? I could just see them in the arcade:

Tony (in a syrupy voice): Oh, no, you *don't* get to put the quarter in the machine.

Rachel (in the same voice): Oh, yes, I *do*.

I was going to Serena's after practice to drop off the tape and hopefully work on the math assignment. Math is something you can talk about without sounding like your lips are stuck in permanent baby-talk mode. I would much rather be with Serena.

When I got to Serena's house, she seemed only a little surprised to see me, and perhaps that was all for show, because this
time her hair was combed and pulled back in clips.

I showed her the tape I'd made and explained what it was.
She took it from my hands and smiled as if I'd just handed her
a Christmas present.

"That's so sweet of you. I'm sure it will really help. If I give
you some blank cassettes, would you mind doing one for me
every day?"

"Sure," I said, and mentally added, I just got a daily invita-
tion to Serena's family room. Try and do that with an airplane,
Brian Vanders.

While I put the tape into the player, Mrs. Kimball brought
in a bowl of popcorn, then left us by ourselves again. I got out
my notes from the day so Serena could follow the examples I'd
talked about on the tape.

She laughed when she heard my sportscaster impersonation on the tape. Shaking her head, she said, "McKay, you're so funny."

One quality down and four left to go before I officially became Mr. Right.

Then we went over the homework assignment. Serena helped me with the first few problems, and I understood them—well, sort of. I understood them while Serena explained them. I couldn't seem to remember how I was supposed to do everything when I tried some problems on my own. So we went back and worked on some earlier stuff I hadn't understood, and it finally made sense. As we finished, I said, "Gee, Serena, I should have crashed into you during PE a long time ago."

Serena picked up a piece of popcorn and threw it at me. "Thanks, McKay. I've sat here bored to death for two days, and you're happy."

I picked up the popcorn, threw it up in the air, and caught it in my mouth. "You don't have to just sit here. Go outside. The weather is great."

She tilted her head to one side. "What am I supposed to do outside? Limp around?"

"There has to be some sports you can play with only one foot." But I couldn't think of any, so I made some up. "There's hopping basketball, and of course crawling baseball, or you could try a really short game of soccer."

Serena threw another piece of popcorn at me.

"You've got a pretty good arm. I bet we could play a game of catch." I took a look around the room. "Do you have a ball somewhere?"

When she realized I was serious, she said, "I don't want to play catch. I'm lousy at sports."

"That's perfect. I'll help you become a great athlete to repay you for helping me with math."

"But you have to move around to play catch."

"No, you won't. I'll throw it right into your lap." She still didn't look convinced, so I added, "Softly. I'll throw the ball very softly because I would hate to send you to the doctor's again."

In the end she gave in. Her mother helped her onto the chaise lounge in the backyard, and she sat with her foot propped up while I threw balls to her. At first she threw them right back to me, but after a while she threw them farther and farther away from me. I ended up running and diving all over her backyard while she sat there and laughed. I didn't mind. Catching wild balls was good practice for baseball; and besides, I liked to hear her laugh.

She said, "McKay, you're almost as good at retrieving balls as our dog."

"Yeah, but I bet your dog can't bat as well as I do."

She nodded. "You're a better batter." Then she giggled at herself and said, "How can you play a game that makes you sound like cookie dough?"

"Baseball is great. As soon as your knee is better, I'll teach you how to hit, too."

"All right," she said. "As soon as my knee is better."

At that moment I liked Serena. It almost made me sad to think that after I did better in math, I wouldn't have a reason to try and hang out with her anymore. Then I stopped feeling sad. I was so bad at math, I figured we'd be together for quite some time.

I was in a great mood until I got home and walked into my room. Legos were strewn on the dresser, over the beds, and from one end of the floor to the other. I kicked through them to put my backpack away, then went to find Kirk. He was lying on the family room floor tying dishcloths to the legs of the couch.

I stood over him and put my hands on my hips. "Kirk, go pick up the mess in our room."

He didn't even look up at me. "I'm still playing with it."

"No, you're not. You're in here attacking the furniture. Now go pick up our room."

"I don't have to, because you're not the boss of me."

I nearly went and stepped on his dish towels just to make him scream, but I didn't want to get my parents mad at me right now. Instead I followed the sound of my dad's voice into the kitchen. My mom was at the cutting board chopping up lettuce, and Dad stood next to her, cutting up tomatoes.

"This is just like sleeping," he teased her. "You take up all the room."

She smiled over at him. "Lettuce is bigger than tomatoes, and besides, you should never complain to a woman who's got a knife."

I went over to them. "My room looks like a Lego bomb went off inside it, and Kirk refuses to clean it up. When are you moving him out?"

Mom sighed and pressed her knife through the lettuce again. "I've got a bunch of transcriptions to do. I don't have time to move everything around."

"I'll help you," I said. "In fact, I volunteer to carry everything to your room."

Another chop to the lettuce. "And then there's the matter of decorating. The office has those old pink curtains and dirt marks all over the wall. It wouldn't be fair to make Kirk move out unless his room is just as nice as the room he came from. I'll need to buy paint, border, curtains, and a comforter. Maybe a matching lamp . . . or some paneling . . . anyway, these things take time."

The humor went out of Dad's voice. "These things also take money. Exactly how much were you planning on spending on all of this?"

Mom stopped chopping and looked over at him. "Why do you always say things like that? It's like you think I just look for excuses to spend money. Do you think it's fair to move Kirk into a bare bedroom?"

"Fair doesn't have anything to do with it. We either have the money in the bank, or we don't. We can't buy things just because we think it's fair."

Mom gave the lettuce a vicious slash. "You're only saying that because you don't care about decorations, but Kirk does."

"You mean you care," Dad said. "Kirk would be just as happy with it if we let him take markers to the walls."

Mom set her knife down on the cutting board a little more forcefully than she needed to. "You know, if I wanted someone to tell me how to use my money all of the time, I'd still be living with my parents." She turned and walked out of the room.

Dad watched her go, took a deep breath, then went back to chopping tomatoes. His mouth was set in a firm line. His knife against the cutting board sounded harsh and crisp.

I stood rooted to the spot, watching my dad, and not knowing what to say. Finally I said, "It's okay, Dad. I guess I can live with Kirk for a while longer."

Dad picked up the cut tomatoes and dropped them into a bowl. Then he picked up what was left of the lettuce and chopped it. "I'm sure it won't be much longer. Your mother will find some irresistible little sports material somewhere, and then she'll be making curtains, comforters, and matching throw pillows." He grumbled something I couldn't hear and then added, "and tablecloths—and place mats."

I started to leave the kitchen, but Dad called me back. "McKay . . ."

I turned toward him, but he didn't say anything else for a moment. He just laid his knife down on the cutting board and folded his arms. Finally he said, "Your mom works hard to make our home a nice place. I didn't mean any of what I just said."

"I know." Besides, I hadn't understood half of what he'd just said anyway.

Now he smiled at me. "You won't have to worry about money when you grow up because you're going to graduate from college and become a corporate executive, right?"

"Right."

"How's the homework coming?"

"Good." For the first time this was true, and I was determined to keep it that way. Suddenly I realized raising my grade wasn't just about baseball. It was about a future my parents saw for me—a future where I didn't have any of the problems that kept troubling them.

Dad nodded. "That's good. Go wash your hands. Dinner is almost ready."

I stopped in the bathroom and washed up, then went into my bedroom and picked up all of the Legos. If the Legos were gone, then the fights would be gone too. But, because I was still mad at Kirk for making the mess in the first place, I put the bucket of Legos on the very top shelf in the closet, where he couldn't reach it.

My parents didn't talk much to each other during dinner. Kirk happily took up the silence by describing the difference between Pikachu and Raichu and which one would win if they ever battled each other.

I was quiet too. I thought about money and how much easier our lives would be if we had just a little more of it.

I had tried, over the last few days, to sell my schoolteachers reverse osmosis systems, but they turned out to be considerably tougher customers than Coach Manetti was. My history,

◇

PE, English, and computer teachers all insisted they already had ROs. My science teacher said he enjoyed the flavor of microbes in his water, and Mrs. Swenson just gave me a long stare and sighed.

"Let me guess," she said. "You don't need to worry about algebra anymore because now you're going to grow up to be a salesman, right?"

"Not at all," I said. "I just thought you'd enjoy the fresh goodness of quality Hendricks water."

She shook her head. "Well, I must admit that a sales job is a more realistic goal than a professional baseball career, but nevertheless, you still have to pass algebra." She glanced down at the grade book on her desk. "You're going to have to do very well on the next unit test if you want to pull your grade up to a C."

"But microorganisms—" I said.

"Please take your seat now," she told me.

And I did.

Now I jabbed my fork into my salad and wished I could make just one more sale—one more sale to someone who wanted a reverse osmosis system now and not later—and then my dad would see it was possible to make money through sales. Mom would have some money to decorate Kirk's room, and everyone would be happy.

But who could I sell an RO to? The neighbors? The bus driver? Strangers I met in the mall? I didn't know a lot of adults, and the ones I did didn't seem to want to take my advice on the dangers of impure water.

There was only one person who I was sure I could sell something to, and that was my grandmother.

After dinner I took the cordless phone to my bedroom and called her. I sat on my bed, nervously drumming my fingers, while I listened to the phone ring. I hoped she was home, and I hoped Kirk didn't walk in during our conversation. Most of all, I hoped I didn't lose my nerve.

"Hello." I heard my grandmother's voice on the other end of the line.

"Hi, Grandma. It's McKay. I was just calling to see how you're doing."

"I'm doing just fine," she said.

"Good, because I love you, and I always want you to be healthy."

"I'm glad to hear that," she said.

"And of course being healthy starts with healthy water."

"Oh?"

"And since we're talking about healthy water, did you know Hendricks now has their very own reverse osmosis system?"

There was a pause on the line and then Grandma said, "Why are you telling me this?"

"Because I want you to be healthy—and because I'm trying to sell reverse osmosis systems for Dad. Do you want to buy one?"

"Not really."

"But it has four patented clear-water filters."

Grandma sounded a little impatient. "McKay, what are you getting out of these sales?"

"Dad gets two hundred dollars."

"I see." There was another pause, and then, "How about I just pay you ten dollars to drop the subject?"

I was persistent. "Oh, come on, Grandma, don't you want clean water?"

"My water is just fine, but if your parents need the money they can call me, and we'll talk about it."

I knew that would never happen. When Grandma came to visit us, my parents didn't even like her to put gas in the car. They'd never accept money from her.

I mumbled, "Well, thanks anyway," and a few other things, and then hung up.

I lay down on my bed, and when I was finished staring at the ceiling, I got the rest of my homework out of my backpack. I saw my algebra book and shoved it farther into my backpack. "Don't worry, Mrs. Swenson," I said out loud. "I'm not about to try for a career as a salesman." I couldn't. I was so bad at it, even my own grandmother wouldn't buy anything from me. All I could do was hope Mom and Dad worked out the details of Kirk's room soon.

Over the next week Tony and Rachel were constantly together. He was at her locker in the morning. She was at his locker before math. I even saw them hold hands outside Mrs. Swenson's room. At baseball practice he gave me a rundown of every phone call they ever had. He always did this in a superior sort of way, like I was supposed to be impressed at what an adult he was.

I still taped the math class and brought it to Serena every day. She helped me with my homework, and we talked about school. It was absolutely the first time in my life I had ever liked algebra. I was getting so good at it, I could actually tell what x was on a regular basis. It may have been my imagination, but it seemed even Mrs. Swenson had a newfound respect for me. Every once in a while, when I passed her on the way to my desk, I'd say, "Go ahead and ask me, just ask me when those trains will meet."

She always told me to sit down, but still, her smile didn't seem quite so dour as she said it.

◇

But the best thing of all was, I felt like Serena and I were becoming friends, and it was a nice comfortable feeling.

Brian, however, was still in the picture. I knew he was either calling or coming over to see Serena because she kept saying things like, "Brian said the pep assembly yesterday was really lame." I could never figure out why she mentioned him to me, or what it all meant. Did she consider Brian, or me, or both of us, as just friends? Did she like one of us as more than a friend? If so, which one? I never tried to find out. To find out meant I had to do something about it, and it was easier to be ignorant and pretend she liked me and was just putting up with Brian.

After a few more days, Serena's knee healed enough that she came back to school, at first on crutches and then without them. We said hi to each other when we passed in the halls, and sometimes I walked her to math class. It was nice to have someone to walk with, since Tony was always goofing off with Rachel outside of the door. Once or twice I saw Brian while I was with Serena. He always glared at me.

I tried not to let it bother me. After all, glaring was not on the list of qualifications for being Mr. Right.

Sometimes Serena and I went over our algebra homework in the library before school, and if I had a problem with anything, she'd help me out. Life had become, for a short moment, a happy peaceful place. Baseball was especially good. We won our last game, which put us in first place in our league. We were ready to take on the other winning teams in our district, and my batting was on fire. Coach Manetti started calling me "the McKay Cannon" because I could smack the ball off in any direction.

All the tournament games were held in a big sports complex in Mesa. Rachel, Anna, and Serena showed up to watch the first one. They sat in the front row of the bleachers and ate popcorn and drank soda. A few times I casually looked over to where they sat, but they never seemed to be watching the game. Mostly they were bent close to one another talking. Every once in a while I'd see them laugh. I hoped they weren't laughing at something we'd done, or at least not something I'd done. Then the game got intense, and I forgot the girls were there altogether.

The Tempe Mavericks were a tough team, and it was touch-and-go until the last inning. We were only one run ahead, and we had to make sure the score stayed that way. When it was all over, we'd won 9 to 8. I had three hits and five runs batted in, and I felt good about that. I was sure our team had looked great on the field, especially me. We gave the other team the standard cheer, then Tony and I gave each other high fives and our usual after-game routine. "Who the man?" he asked me.

"You the man."

"You the man," he said back to me.

We walked toward the bleachers and noticed the girls standing behind the backstop, waiting for us.

"Good game!" Serena called. "You made a great hit, McKay."

I was glad she'd seen that happen.

"And you were super, too, Tony," Rachel added.

"Yeah, Tony," Anna cooed. "I was very impressed by your moves."

They went on congratulating us for a few more minutes, but my mind was stuck on Anna's first comment. Something about the way she said it bothered me, and as I watched her I became more and more sure I was right. Anna looked at Tony. Anna smiled at Tony. Anna laughed at everything Tony said, even the stupid stuff. It all meant one thing. Anna liked Tony.

I never mentioned my observation about Anna to anyone. I mean, what would I have said? "Hey, Tony, you'd better tone down that walk. You're attracting too many girls."

Or to Serena: "Hey, what is it with your friends? How come they all like Tony so much instead of, say, me?"

Or to Anna herself: "You might not have ever walked past Mrs. Swenson's room at math time, but in case you didn't know, Tony is taken." Of course Anna knew Tony was taken. It was her friend, Rachel, who took him.

I didn't want to get involved in the whole thing. And I wouldn't have, if everyone didn't drag me into it.

It happened the next week at the school dance. I had never been to one of the school dances before, and I hadn't ever planned on going to one until they did something besides dance at them. I mean, who invented dancing? It wasn't a guy, that's for sure. A guy would never voluntarily choose to stand in front of his friends and peers waving his arms around like he's trying to flag down an invisible boat in the next room. Girls invented dancing. I know they did. Back in prehistoric times all of the cavewomen got together and decided to play a huge practical joke on the cavemen.

They said, "We've discovered something called dancing. Stand here and wave your arms around while everyone watches you. It will be fun."

And men have been stuck dancing ever since.

So I was firmly against going to the dance, but Tony wanted to go, and he kept insisting I come with him. As we sat on the bench waiting to bat during game two of the tournament, he brought up the subject again.

"You'll have a good time."

"I don't want to ask a girl to dance. What if she says no?"

"Then you ask someone else."

"What if they *all* say no?"

Tony stretched out his legs and shrugged. "They won't all say no. In the history of school dances, I don't think that's ever happened."

But I might be that lucky first one.

"Besides," Tony said with a grin, "Serena will say yes."

Until that moment I had forgotten Serena would be going. At least, I hoped she'd go. She and her friends hadn't come to see us play game two, but how many games could you expect a girl to sit through when she didn't fully understand the concept of baseball? I was still surprised that she'd shown up for game one. As I got up to take my turn to bat, I said, "Well, all right, I guess I could give the dance a try."

We won the game 8 to 6. It was a great afternoon. The McKay Cannon was in action, and I was invincible.

The dance was that Friday night in the school auditorium. I had thought there would be decorations of some sort, but it was just the auditorium with a sound system on the stage and the bleachers pulled halfway across the gym floor to create a dance area. At first when Tony and I walked in, I could barely see anything because it was so dark. But after a few moments I could tell which kids were on the dance floor (mostly couples, because it was a slow dance) and which kids sat on the bleachers (everybody else). A few parents were also perched on the top rows of the bleachers. I guess they were the chaperones.

We were in front of the speakers, so Tony said to me, in a voice that was close to shouting, "Let's go over to the bleachers and see if Rachel is here."

"Okay!" I yelled back.

We walked over to the bleachers, and after a few moments of searching, we saw Anna sitting by herself. She waved us over, and Tony and I sat down beside her.

"Where are Rachel and Serena?" Tony asked her. He didn't have to yell anymore because we were far enough away from the speakers that we could almost carry on a normal conversation.

"They're both out dancing," Anna said, and I noticed she scooted a little closer to Tony.

Tony looked a bit astonished. "Rachel's slow dancing with another guy?"

Anna shrugged and smiled at him. "Loyalty isn't Rachel's strong point."

Apparently it wasn't Anna's strong point either, because she scooted even closer to Tony. "Do you want to dance?" she asked.

Tony took another look out on the dance floor and then turned back to Anna. "Sure." The two of them got up and left me without another word.

So there I was. Alone on the bleachers with a roomful of modern-day cavewomen all just waiting to watch me flail around and make a fool of myself. At least it was dark. I bet guys invented dance-floor lighting. The prehistoric cavemen had said, "We'll dance if we have to, but we won't do it in the light of day."

I moved up the bleachers in an attempt to be farther away from the dancing. If I was high enough up, nobody would ask me to dance; and I could just spend the night casually observing all the rest of my fellow cavemen. Since it was a slow song, nobody was actually flailing around at this point. They all just stood there, swaying a little. Swaying didn't look too hard. I could probably manage to sway as well as anybody else, but if I asked a girl to dance during a slow song, what would she think?

Also, were you supposed to talk to each other while you danced? If so, what were you supposed to talk about? I felt a small bolt of panic run through me as I realized I didn't know the answer to these questions. I should have asked Tony what exactly one was supposed to do while dancing, but now it was too late. He was out swaying with Anna, and if anyone asked me to dance now, I'd mess up for sure.

I moved a couple more bleacher steps up. From there I could see Serena dancing with Brian. I wondered whether Serena had asked him to dance, or whether he'd asked her. It was hard to tell whether she was enjoying the dance or not, since it was so dark, and I couldn't see her face clearly.

What if Serena spent every dance with him, and I had absolutely no one I wanted to dance with? I wondered if Tony would mind if I left without him, or whether my parents would mind coming to get me ten minutes after they'd dropped me off. Then the song ended, and Tony, Anna, Rachel, and Serena all came back to the bleachers. Brian, happily, was nowhere to be seen. I went down and stood with them. I didn't hear the first part of their conversation, but when I got there, it was clear Tony and Rachel weren't happy with each other. Rachel had her arms crossed and said, "Well, if you hadn't come late, you could have asked me to dance instead."

Tony said, "What? You couldn't wait a few minutes for me?"

Rachel rolled her eyes. "Why are you so upset? It's not that big a deal."

"Fine," Tony said. "Then it won't be a big deal when I ask someone else to dance the next slow dance."

"That's fine with me," Rachel said crisply.

"Fine," Tony repeated. They both looked out at the dance floor and not at each other.

Serena, Anna, and I all stared at each other silently for a moment, then Serena said, "Come on, you guys, stop fighting. Let's all go out and dance."

"Yeah, let's," Anna said. She was glancing over at Tony.

Serena grabbed my hand and pulled me out onto the floor. Tony and Rachel grudgingly followed us, and Anna followed them. Serena walked to an empty spot on the floor, then began dancing. She looked smooth and self-confident, but of course, she would have looked that way doing anything. I'm afraid I looked like I was trying to stomp out a fire. I still wasn't sure if I was supposed to say anything while I was dancing or not. Tony wasn't saying anything, but that may have been because he was mad. I hoped Serena didn't think I was mad just because I wasn't talking.

The song ended, and another one started. No one made any moves to leave the floor, so I kept dancing too. I tried to be more creative with my dance moves, but I most likely looked like a guy who was not only trying to stomp out a fire, but also trying to punch someone out in the process.

Then a slow song came on. I looked over at Serena. She looked back at me. I cleared my throat and took a step toward her. Out of the corner of my eye I saw Tony take Anna's hand and say, "Come on, let's dance."

Rachel stood watching them for a moment. Then her lips pressed together to form an angry frown. She grabbed my hand and said, "Let's dance, McKay."

What could I do? Rachel had already put her hand on my shoulder and was getting into "sway" position. I looked over at Serena to see what her reaction to all of this was, but she'd already turned and was walking toward the bleachers. Before she got there, Brian intercepted her. They talked for a moment. She smiled up at him, and then he led her back onto the floor. They went up toward the front of the room and melted into the rest of the crowd, so I couldn't see them anymore. I swayed slowly back and forth with Rachel and hoped Brian broke something during the next football game.

I still wasn't sure whether or not I was supposed to say anything while I danced, so I leaned closer to Rachel and said, "It's a nice song, huh?"

She grunted out something that sounded like, "Huwuff," and I figured she wasn't in the mood for conversation. I didn't try to say anything else. Besides, it was for the best that we were quiet. If she had said anything, it most likely would have been something bad about Tony. Maybe he deserved it, but Tony was my best friend, and you've got to stand by your best friend even when he acts like a jerk.

Ahh, that old Manetti charm.

I glanced over at Tony and Anna. They were dancing really close and talking. Anna's face was tipped up toward him, and she was laughing at something he said. Probably something stupid.

When the song ended, Rachel didn't say anything to me at all. She just turned and walked toward the gym door. I looked over at Tony to see if he'd go and get her, but he only watched her for a second and then turned back to Anna. Rachel was almost to the door before I saw Serena break away from the crowd and go after her.

Tony and Anna stayed out on the dance floor, but I went back to the bleachers and sat down. After a few minutes a girl from my social studies class asked me to dance. Then after that a girl from my church found me, and I danced a couple of dances with her. All in all, quite a sample of the girls in my grade got to see me do my stomp-fire, punch-someone routine. Somewhere in heaven I'm sure a bunch of cavewomen got a good laugh.

I kept an eye out for Serena but didn't see her again until about an hour later. She walked back into the gym, but Rachel wasn't with her. I had been sitting on the bleachers talking to a couple of guys, but I got up when I saw her.

A slow song started to play. It was perfect timing. I walked toward Serena, and when she saw me, she waved for me to come over. As I got close to her she said, "There you are, McKay. I have something to ask you."

"I have something to ask you too." It's funny, but at that moment I wasn't worried about asking Serena to dance at all. I was just relieved she hadn't left.

"Probably the same thing," she said. But instead of going out to the dance floor, she motioned for me to walk with her toward the door. I followed her out of the gymnasium, and we stood in the hallway.

She leaned against the wall and sighed. "Rachel is really upset."

"Oh, sorry to hear that." She looked at me like she expected me to say more, but I wasn't sure what. I mean, what could I do about Rachel being upset?

"What has Tony said to you?" Serena asked.

"Nothing."

She tilted her head in question, so I added, "I haven't talked to him. He's been busy dancing."

"Oh." She seemed surprised by this, like she'd thought that after their fight, Tony and I had immediately gotten together and discussed our feelings about relationships and life. Maybe that's what she and Rachel had just done.

Serena took a folded piece of notebook paper out of her pocket and gave it to me. "It's a note from Rachel. Can you give it to Tony the next time you see him?"

"Okay." I put the note in my pocket.

Serena cocked her head again and said, "So if you didn't have any messages from Tony, what was it you wanted to ask me?"

"Oh, that." Suddenly I felt awkward. I was out in the hallway where the lights were bright, and we were all alone. "I was going to ask you to dance."

"Oh." She smiled, and for some reason I felt completely transparent. I felt like she could look into my mind and see what I was thinking. "Sure," she said, "let's dance."

We walked back into the gymnasium, and I took her hand in mine. As we danced, I took small steps to make absolutely certain I didn't step on her feet. I was standing so close to her, I could tell her hair smelled like strawberries, and I wondered why it is that girls always smell so good. The song was almost over when we'd come in, so we only got to dance for a total of about forty-five seconds, but it was still a nice forty-five seconds. After the song ended, Serena looked up at me and said, "I probably ought to get back to Rachel. She went to call her mom, and I'm riding home with her."

I nodded and said, "I guess I'll see you at math class."

She turned around to leave, but then turned back to me. "You want to get together after school on Monday to do our homework?"

"Yeah, that would be great."

"All right. I'll meet you after school by the front door, and we'll walk over to my house."

I watched her leave, then turned back to the dance floor. An upbeat song was playing, and I sung along under my breath. Dances, I thought, were not so bad after all.

I danced a few more dances; then after the last song was over, Tony came and found me so we could ride home together. He was still with Anna. I knew they hadn't been together the whole time because I'd seen him dancing with other girls, but she was with him now. She walked over with Tony to where I stood and then said, "Well, see you at school, Tony." And she dragged out the word "Tony" until it sounded like she was saying, "Toe-neeee."

Tony gave her a smile and said, "See you later, Anna."

I waited until she'd walked out the door and then said, "That reminds me. Serena gave me this to give to you. It's from Rachel." I took the note out of my pocket and handed it to him.

He unfolded it, but then said, "It's too dark here to read," so we went into the hallway. He took a minute to read it, then folded it back up and put it in his pocket.

"She's mad at me, and she's not sure if we should go out anymore." He shook his head. "What's that supposed to mean? Does she think she deserves some big apology or something? It's not my fault she ran out of the gym. I was going to ask her to dance the next slow dance, but she took off. After all, she's the one who said it was no big deal to slow-dance with some-one else." At this point he looked to me as though he expected me to chime in and agree with him.

"Uh, yeah," I said. "She did say that."

"I wanted her to know how it feels to see your date with someone else."

We walked slowly down the hallway and out toward the parking lot. I tried to keep my voice low so no one would over-hear us. "You danced with Anna a lot."

"Yeah," Tony said, "She's really cute, and I think she likes me. She kind of, you know, looks at me a lot." He was silent for a moment and then said, "Anna seems nicer than Rachel. Do you think I should break up with Rachel and ask Anna to go out with me?"

"Rachel and Anna are friends."

Tony got a big smile across his face. "I know, but I'm almost sure Anna would go out with me anyway."

"But don't you think Rachel would get mad at Anna if she went out with you?"

Tony shrugged. "It's not my fault Rachel is being mean and

Anna is being nice. I didn't tell Rachel to write this note. She's practically already broken up with me. It would serve her right if I asked out her friend."

I pushed open the door, and we walked out into the warm evening air. "Tony," I said, "I think it's my duty as your best friend to tell you you're being a jerk."

Tony laughed like he thought I was joking. "Just because you date one girl doesn't mean you can't ever date any of her friends. Girls understand that. They do it too. It's all part of the game—all part of playing the field. You'll understand when you start dating."

I wanted to say, "Tony, now you're being an even bigger jerk," but I didn't. He obviously thought he was the authority when it came to women, and he wouldn't listen to me anyway. Besides, maybe he was right. Maybe even as we stood in the school parking lot waiting for my parents to pick us up, Rachel and Anna were somewhere talking about Tony. Maybe they were discussing trading him like baseball teams traded around players.

Rachel was saying, "Okay, you can have Tony, but I get to borrow your new blue sweater whenever I want to."

"All right," Anna answered. "But when I'm finished with Tony, I get my sweater back too, unless of course I want to borrow another boyfriend from you."

Maybe dating in junior high was always just like playing a game. You won by getting someone new to like you. Only I hated to think of it that way.

Tony said, "Then again, maybe I should try to work things out with Rachel. After all we have been going out for a few weeks. I don't know. I guess I'll call them both tomorrow and see who's nicer to me."

I didn't get the chance to comment on his methods of choosing a girlfriend, because just then we saw my dad pull up in his truck. But I did wonder, as I climbed into the front seat, if my dad had ever decided on a girlfriend by calling a couple of girls to see who was nicest to him. I hoped not.

9

*A*t school on Monday, I hardly talked to Serena at all, except for the time she gave me another note to give to Tony. Before we walked into math class, she slipped me a folded piece of notebook paper. With a serious expression on her face she said, "It's from Rachel. She needs to talk to Tony."

I said, "All right, I'll give it to him," and then handed it to Tony as I sat down at my desk.

He looked over at me. "Who's this from?"

"Rachel."

He read it silently, then shook his head. "She's so dramatic."

"I guess this means Anna was nicer to you on the phone."

"Yeah, I guess she was, but I still don't know what I'll do." He shrugged as though it didn't matter a whole lot to him and got out his books.

I glanced over at Serena's seat. She was watching Tony with the same serious expression she'd had when she talked to me.

* * *

I waited for ten minutes at the school's front door before Serena showed up. I had almost decided she'd forgotten we were getting together to study when she walked out the door with her backpack.

"Sorry I'm late," she told me. "I was talking to Anna and Rachel."

"Oh." I headed down the steps with her. We walked silently for a few minutes, but I could tell by the way Serena kept glancing over at me that she expected me to say something. I just wasn't sure what.

After a few more moments of her giving me "the glance," I decided talking about anything would be better than walking all the way to her house in silence. "We've got game three of the tournament tomorrow," I told her. "We play the team from Queen Creek. Their star pitcher just had to move to California because his dad got a job transfer. Queen Creek's loss—our gain. Coach Manetti says it should be an easy win."

Serena walked beside me on the sidewalk, but didn't look over at me. "Is he a good coach?"

"He's the best in the league."

"Is he nice, though?"

This just goes to show you what girls know about coaching. "He's tough. That's why he's the best."

"Oh." She looked contemplative. "I was just wondering about Tony."

"Wondering what?"

We had reached Serena's house. As we went up the walk, she said, "I was wondering what kind of family Tony comes from."

I shrugged. "A normal family, I guess. Why?"

"I just wonder why he acts the way he does."

I had no idea what she was talking about. As we walked through the door I said, "Acts what way?"

Serena shrugged and I followed her into the kitchen. We set our backpacks on the table, and I thought she'd finished with the subject of Tony, but while we got our books out, she said, "You know, why he would simultaneously go after two girls who *used to be* best friends."

Now I understood. We were talking about that old Manetti charm. "I don't think Tony is actually going after Anna. . . ."

Serena opened her algebra book so hard the cover thunked against the table. "He called her on Saturday, and he talked to her today in the hallway. She said he was really nice." Serena said the words *really nice* like it was a criminal offense.

"Well, that's probably because Anna was really nice to him first."

Serena gasped at this as though it were an accusation. "She was not."

"Yes, she was."

"How has she been nice?"

"Well . . ." I was at a disadvantage in defending Tony. We'd only talked about Anna in a general sort of way, but it was clear Serena knew every detail of both of her friend's love lives. "She looks at him," I said. "A lot."

"She looks at him?"

"Yeah, you know, the way girls look at a guy when they want to be noticed."

"She looks at him?" Serena said again.

"You're a girl. You must know 'the look.'"

Serena's eyes narrowed. This was not the look I had in mind. "Your friend Tony is not only a two-timing jerk, he's an egotistical jerk too. He thinks just because a girl looks at him, she's interested?"

"Oh, come on, you can't tell me Anna isn't interested in Tony."

"This isn't Anna's fault. Tony is just using her to get Rachel upset."

I leaned forward over my math book. "Anna was practically chasing Tony. If you're going to be mad at him, you have to be mad at Anna too."

Serena shut her math book with a slam. "I don't think I feel like studying algebra today."

"Or," I said, "you can just be mad at me." I picked up my book and shoved it back into my backpack. Then I stood up so quickly that I nearly knocked over the chair. I was halfway across the kitchen when she called after me. "McKay, I'm sorry. I didn't mean to take it out on you."

She ran one hand across her hair and gave me a half shrug. "I know it's not your fault Rachel and Anna are fighting. I mean, you didn't tell Tony to go after both of them." Then, a little less certainly, she added, "Did you?"

"Like I could ever tell Tony what to do."

"Are we friends again?"

"Sure."

She looked at me—and it was that girl look I was talking about earlier. "I still don't want to study algebra."

"What do you want to do then?"

She raised her shoulders, then relaxed them, but didn't say anything.

"Let's go outside and play catch," I suggested.

"Don't you ever think about anything besides baseball?"

"Remember, I promised I'd help you learn to play, and this is the perfect time to practice."

She smiled, so I knew she didn't mind catch so much after all. "All right, Coach, I'll work on it."

We found an old tennis ball in the hall closet, then went to her backyard, and I instructed her on throwing balls overhand with proper form.

"It feels funny," she said as she flung the ball at me.

I caught the ball with one hand. "You'll get used to it. I mean, you don't want to go through life throwing like a girl, do you?"

"I am a girl."

"Really?" I tossed the ball back to her. "I hadn't noticed."

"Yeah, I figured as much." She nearly caught the ball, but it bounced from her hands and onto the grass.

As she bent down to pick it up, I said, "What's that supposed to mean?"

◇

"Nothing." She threw the ball so high I had to jump for it.

We threw the ball for a few more minutes, and this time she caught them all.

"See," I told her, "it's not so hard."

"Well, it's not hard with you, but it's a lot harder in PE when I'm playing an actual game, and the ball is coming toward me and everyone stares at me."

"They're not staring at you, they're staring at the ball."

"And everyone always moves up when I come to bat. It's totally embarrassing."

"You'll surprise everyone next game."

We played for a while longer, and then Serena's mom came outside. "I thought you two were supposed to be doing homework," she said.

So we went back inside and got out our books again. We ate chips and did the problems by ourselves, then checked our answers. We came up with different numbers for two of the problems, so we reworked those together. It was basically Serena showing me where I'd messed up, but I understood it once she'd gone over it with me, so I felt good about it.

"See," she said. "Algebra isn't so hard."

"Well, it's not hard with you. It's a lot harder in math class when I'm doing an actual problem and everyone is staring at me. Everyone looks up when I go to the chalkboard. It's totally embarrassing."

Serena picked up a Dorito and threw it at me, overhand, which just goes to show you she was taking my throwing lessons to heart. We goofed off for a little while longer, then I told Serena I'd better go or my parents would get after me. She walked me to the door. Right before I left, I turned back to face her and gave her a studious look. "Hey," I said, "You're a girl."

She tilted her head at me in mock surprise. "You noticed."

"Yeah, I guess you could say I did." I gave her a half wave and went out the door.

I walked home slowly. For the first time in my life I thought that no-dating-until-you're-sixteen rule was really stupid.

I walked a while longer and wondered if Serena would understand if I asked her out on a date, but then told her she'd have to wait three years for me to come pick her up.

Probably not.

I suppose I could just bend that dating rule a little. I'd tell my parents I was going out with Tony, but wouldn't mention I was also going to be with Serena and Rachel. Or Anna, depending on who Tony decided on. And we wouldn't call it a date. We'd call it "doing something with friends." Certainly I could "do something with friends" before I was sixteen. That is, if my parents never found out about it.

But then what came next? I couldn't just ask her out once and then never ask her out again. I'd have to think of other things to ask her to do with me. How many activities could I come up with that wouldn't involve driving, that wouldn't cost a lot of money, and that I'd be able to keep secret from my parents? I'd always been lousy at keeping things from my parents, and the thought of suddenly living a double life didn't exactly

◇

appeal to me. It would involve a lot of creatively stretching the truth, a lot of tense and stressful moments, and most likely some really big punishment at the end.

The best thing to do was to avoid all of the stress and just convince my parents I was old enough to do things with girls now. I just needed to reason with them. Reason would work. And flattery always helped.

When I got home, I found my mother in the office, typing on the computer.

I went and stood beside her desk. "Hi, Mom, I'm home." I waited for a second and then added. "Your hair looks very nice today."

She eyed me suspiciously. "And I suppose my car is always very tidy too."

"Yes, in fact, it is."

Mom stopped typing. "Look, McKay, I'm almost finished with Dr. Warren's transcripts, and then I'll have time to think about moving the office. Until then you'll just have to wait for privacy."

"I'm sure you're doing your best."

"I'm glad you think so." Mom went back to her typing. I stood by and watched her for a moment. I tried to think of a logical, reasonable way to put forth my argument.

"You know, I think kids these days are a lot more mature than they were when you grew up," I said.

Mom's fingers continued to click away at the keyboard. "You do, do you?"

"What with all of the technology, and TV programs, and computers—we just grow up earlier."

"Uh-huh." She still typed, but her pace was getting slower, so I knew she was listening.

"I guess it isn't surprising that teenagers have started dating earlier too."

"I guess it's not."

"So although that no-dating-until-you're-sixteen rule was probably a good idea when you were young, it's outdated for today's kids, don't you think?"

Mom stopped typing and turned in her chair until she faced me. "No, I don't. As you said, today's kids have a lot of pressures, a lot of temptations, a lot of 'life' to deal with. The last thing you need is to try and deal with relationships on top of all of that. I think that no-dating-until-you're-sixteen rule is more important than ever."

I stared at her in surprise, then abandoned reason and said the first thing that came to my mind. "But all of the kids my age are going out."

Mom returned her attention to the keyboard. "Sometimes being different is good for you."

"But it's a stupid rule. Why do I have to wait until I'm sixteen?"

"Because thirteen-year-olds aren't mature enough to date."

I glared at her for a moment. "You don't think I'm mature?"

She didn't answer.

"You know I go over to Serena's house to study sometimes.

How come I'm mature enough to study with her but not mature enough to go see a movie with her?"

"Because one you do as a friend and the other you do as a boyfriend."

I threw up my hands. "Don't you like Serena?"

Mom stopped typing and turned toward me. "I barely even know Serena. That isn't the point. If you want to be friends with a girl, that's fine. If you want to study together, that's even better. I hope you study with Serena all through college—it would do wonders for your grade-point average—but right now you're not mature enough to pair off with girls. And that's the end of the discussion." Mom turned back to the computer and began typing again, and this time I knew the discussion was over.

It wasn't fair. It wasn't fair, but I knew if I said anything else, it would just get me in trouble.

I turned, walked from the room, and slammed the door behind me. As I went through the family room, I saw one of Kirk's stuffed animals on the floor. With a swift kick, I hurled it into the kitchen. I didn't see Dad standing in the hallway until he spoke. Then, with his hands on his hips, he said, "Hey, what is this slamming and kicking all about?"

"Mom doesn't think I'm mature!" I said, and stomped off to my room.

Once there I lay on my bed, ripped out little pieces of paper from my science notebook, and threw them across the room.

Of course my parents didn't think I was mature. They probably still thought of me as eight years old. They made me share a room with my five-year-old brother. They didn't believe me when I told them I'd sold a reverse osmosis—I'd done something even my dad hadn't done, and he wouldn't even believe me about it. Of course they thought I was too young to date. They'd *always* think I was too young to date. I'd be forty years old and in the Baseball Hall of Fame before my parents considered me mature enough to socialize.

I took an extra-big wad of paper and hurled it at the mirror on my closet door.

Just what were my parents afraid I was going to do if I went out with Serena anyway? Certainly they trusted me—did they not trust her? Maybe they thought girls were a bad influence or something. One date with Serena, and suddenly I'd be dressing like a hoodlum and in the middle of a drug-smuggling ring in Columbia.

But that was just the point. My parent's didn't know Serena. If they did know her—then certainly they'd change their minds about everything. They'd see what a nice girl she was and realize nothing bad would happen if we went out. All I had to do was arrange for my parents to spend some time with her. I'd invite Serena over to study at my house, and I'd make sure my mother came in and talked to her. Once Mom got to know Serena, Mom would adore her. She'd *want* Serena around. And then it would be no trouble at all to convince my parents it was a good idea for Serena and I to go out.

Then all I'd have to do was convince Serena of the same thing.

10

The next day at school, between every period, I either delivered a note to Tony or took one from him to Serena for Rachel. Serena always wore a worried expression during all this note-passing, like she found the whole thing very distressing.

I had meant to ask her the first time I saw her if she wanted to come over to my house and study for the math test we were having on Thursday, but somehow I didn't. I couldn't.

I knew it was silly. After all, Serena and I had studied together a lot, it shouldn't have been hard to ask her to my house. Especially since I was considering asking her out. But every time I looked at her, the words got stuck in the back of my throat. What if she said no? What if she didn't like me after all? What if she really had a thing for flying football players?

After the third note, I finally got up my courage. As I handed her the latest "for Rachel" note, I said, "Are you ready for the algebra test?"

Serena slipped the folded piece of paper into her notebook. "I think so."

"Do you want to study anyway?"

"I always study anyway," she said, as though it were a stupid question.

"No, I mean, do you want to study with me?"

"Ohhh," she said.

Was that an unhappy oh? Was that an I'd-rather-not-but-I'm-not-sure-how-to-say-no oh?

"When were you thinking?" she asked.

"I don't have ball practice on Wednesday. We could go to my house after school."

Serena considered this for a moment. "I'm not sure if I can. I think Rachel said she wanted to go to the mall on Wednesday."

"Oh. Okay." My neck felt hot, and suddenly I found that I had to gulp, but I tried to act like it didn't matter. "Maybe some other time."

"Let me talk to Rachel about it," Serena said, "and then I'll let you know for sure."

Great. Another chance to be formally rejected. "Okay," I said. I nodded out a good-bye, then walked to Tony's locker. He was just putting away his science stuff and getting his English books out.

"Here." I handed him the note and walked off. It bothered me, it really did, that even in the middle of all his girl problems, Tony's love life was still better than mine.

By the time I got to algebra I'd delivered two more notes. It didn't even faze me when the guy beside me handed me a folded piece of paper and whispered, "It's from Serena."

Without thinking about it, I passed the note on to Tony. He opened it, gave me a funny look, then leaned over and handed it back to me.

"I think it's for you," he said. "Either that, or Serena is the latest victim of the Manetti charm."

Not likely. I glanced over at Serena to see if she'd seen me hand the paper to Tony. She was shaking her head.

I opened it and read, "Rachel wants to go to the mall in the evening, so after school will be fine to study."

I turned and mouthed the word *okay* to Serena, then I took the paper and put it in my math folder. A few other miscellaneous notes were crammed inside, and I made a mental note to take the notes out of my folder and put them in my dresser when I got home. Now that I was getting notes from girls, I didn't want any of them to fall out, or fall into the wrong hands.

During dinner that night, I announced my study arrangements. "It's not a date," I told my mother pointedly. "If we were planning to do anything fun, you could veto it, but we're just studying algebra."

Mom took a drink from her glass. "Ah, this subject again." She looked over at my father. "It's your turn to tell him the reason why he can't date. He obviously doesn't listen to me."

Dad cut through his piece of chicken and took a bite. When

he'd finished chewing, he looked at me and said, "You can't date because I said so, and I don't need a reason, because I'm your father."

Mom cut a piece of her own chicken. "Thanks. I'm sure that cleared it up for him."

"She's a really nice girl," I said. "And she's a straight-A student. That means she's a positive influence on me."

"All good qualities in a friend," Mom said.

"You'll probably think she's wonderful once she comes over and you get to know her better. I mean, I bet she'll remind you of your old friends, or your sisters, or someone you liked a whole lot."

Mom took another drink.

"Did I mention she is a straight-A student?"

Mom glanced over at Dad with an exasperated look, but he quickly took another bite of his chicken so he didn't have to say anything.

Mom tapped a finger against the table for a moment, then looked over at me with that parent-lecturing look. "You want to be Serena's friend for the long run, don't you?"

"Sure."

"Then stop thinking about dating her. At your age that's the fastest way to ruin a friendship."

"Why?"

"It just is. You'll understand when you get older."

I hated it when my parents said that. I was convinced it was just something old people said when they couldn't think of any reasons to defend their point of view. They figured we'd forget

◇

about all these explanations as time went by. I decided to start making a list.

The telephone rang, and Dad went into the kitchen to answer it. I ate my chicken silently and let Kirk jabber on about kindergarten. It was pointless to push the topic any farther with Mom. I was just going to have to wait until Serena came over to my house and Mom got to see what an intelligent, mature, and responsible person she was.

Dad came back to the table, smiling and shaking his head. "Well, McKay, I have to admit it. You were right. Mr. Manetti just called and volunteered to buy a reverse osmosis from me."

I smiled back at him. "See. I told you he would. When do you get the two hundred dollars?"

"Well, I didn't actually sell him a Hendricks RO."

"That's true. So when do I get the two hundred dollars?"

Dad laughed. "No, I mean I told him to go down to Home Depot and pick up one there. They're not quite as fancy as the Hendricks systems, but they do the job. No sense in paying twice the money for one."

I stared at him as though he hadn't said this, as though in just a moment he'd tell me he was joking. "You told him what?"

"He was a little worried he wouldn't be able to install it himself, but I told him I'd come over and put it in for him."

"You told him what?"

"What are you surprised about, McKay? You're the one who told him he should get an RO in the first place."

"But not a Home Depot RO," I said. "He was supposed to buy a Hendricks RO so you could get the bonus."

Dad cocked his head in surprise. "You wouldn't want your coach to pay extra for something just so I can make a few bucks, would you?"

Yes, I would. Only I didn't say it. Saying it out loud would make me sound as selfish as I suddenly felt. The truth was, the Manettis had plenty of money, and we didn't. Why shouldn't they buy a Hendricks RO?

I looked over at Mom to see her reaction to this. Mom, who always complained there wasn't enough to account for in the bank account, didn't seem disturbed at all that Dad had just thrown away two hundred dollars. She calmly took another bite of her salad.

Dad went on, "You don't make money off your friends, son. Friends help one another out."

"I know," I said. "And Coach Manetti was helping us out."

"We don't need that kind of help," Dad said.

I looked over at Mom again. She nodded in agreement. Two hundred dollars would have bought a lot of paint and curtain material for the office, but she was still nodding.

All right. My parents didn't want to feel like a charity case. I could understand that. But still, all was not lost. I shrugged back my shoulders and said, "Well, I guess I can see why you don't want to sell an RO to Coach Manetti, but that doesn't mean you can't sell ROs to anyone else, does it?"

"Nobody else has called for one."

I kept my voice even to make Dad realize I was serious. "It wouldn't be that hard for you to sell a few ROs every once in a while, would it?"

Dad put his fork down. "McKay, why is it you suddenly want me to sell ROs?"

"So you can get the bonuses."

"And why do you think I need those?"

"You know, so you can buy more stuff, and so you and Mom will stop worrying about money all of the time."

Dad looked over at Mom. She blushed a little and said, "We don't worry about money all of the time." Now Dad and I both looked over at her. She sat up a little straighter in her chair. "What?" she said.

Neither Dad nor I answered.

She put down her fork. "All right, I admit it, sometimes I talk about wanting more money, but everyone does that. It doesn't mean I think we're destitute."

"Well, apparently our son thinks it," Dad said. His brows furrowed together for a moment as though something had just occurred to him. "McKay, would these worries of yours happen to have anything to do with the fact that Grandma sent us a check for two hundred dollars in a just-thinking-about-you card?"

"Uh, well, maybe. I did try to sell her a reverse osmosis a while back."

Dad put his face in his hands, then looked over at my mother. "I told you it wasn't early senility. I told you we should have called and asked her what it was all about." He shook his head. "You get to call and tell her we're not homeless yet."

"Don't blame me for all of this," she told him. "I'm not the only one who complains about money. You're the one who makes an issue every time I buy anything."

"You're doing it again," I said. "You're fighting about money."

Dad ran his fingers over his head and then sighed. He glanced over at Mom, then back at me. "Maybe we do argue about money sometimes, and maybe we wish we had more. But nobody has enough money for all of their wants. We have enough for our needs, though, and that's what's important."

"But it wouldn't hurt to have a little more every once in a while, would it? Tony's dad could teach you how to sell stuff. He's really good at it." And then to prove the point I added, "He drives a BMW."

Dad shook his head slightly. "I'm not a salesman, son. I could never do it. I'd hate to feel like I'm pushing something on someone that they don't really want. That's just not me."

"And I'm glad it's not you." Mom smiled over at him. "You're the type of person who is always genuine, and I love you for it." Now she smirked at him. "Even if you don't drive a BMW."

Dad grunted. "It would be a little awkward to lug all my tools around in a sports car."

And then they both laughed. It was nice to see them that way, and I told myself to remember that for every time they fought about money, there were also these times they joked about it. It made me feel better, even though I knew we would never have a BMW, or a bigger house.

*T*hat night, while Tony and I warmed up on the outfield before the game with Queen Creek, I noticed Anna sit down on the front row of the bleachers. "Hey, Tony," I said, "part of your fan club is here."

He looked over to where she sat and waved. She smiled and waved back.

When we finished with warm-ups, we still had a few minutes before the game began, so we walked over to say hi.

"Where are Serena and Rachel?" I asked.

Anna shrugged. "I don't know, at home, I guess." Which meant she had come on her own, and they didn't know she was here.

I didn't say anything else. I just stood by stiffly and listened while Anna and Tony smiled and talked to each other about the game. Anna giggled a lot. She also wished Tony good luck three times.

I thought back to my conversation with Serena, when I

couldn't come up with proof that Anna was chasing Tony. This was proof, and yet I still couldn't make my point. To tell Serena about Anna's visit seemed too much like tattling.

After a few more minutes of watching Tony be funny, honest, attractive, understanding, and loyal—well, maybe not loyal—I decided Anna and Tony were too wrapped up in talking to each other to care whether I was standing there or not. I saw my family sitting a little way off in the bleachers, so I went over to talk to them. Dad gave me his usual pep talk: "You can win this game, son. Just play hard and concentrate."

Mom told me, "Remember, it doesn't matter if you win or not, so long as you do your best."

Kirk said, "When those guys run past you"—he made jogging arm motions to make sure I understood—"trip them."

"That wouldn't be fair," Mom told him.

"Then how about you push them?" Kirk said.

Finally, Coach Manetti told the team to take our seats on the bench, and I forgot all about who was or wasn't in the crowd. That is, until we came to bat in the top of the second inning. Then I glanced up at the bleachers and noticed not only Anna sitting there, but also Rachel and Serena. And none of them looked very happy. Rachel's arms were crossed, and she was tapping her foot quickly against the bleacher. Anna sat a little apart from the other two and stared blankly at the field. Serena just looked uncomfortable, and no one was speaking to anyone else.

"Tony," I said. "Did you notice the rest of your fan club showed up?"

"Yeah," he said, but he didn't sound enthusiastic about the fact. A couple of minutes later he went up to bat and missed two easy pitches. I held my breath while the pitcher threw the third pitch. The ball flew toward the plate, a little high, but probably still within the strike zone. Tony swung and missed again. He tossed his head back, groaned, and then dropped the bat a little less gently than he should have. He walked slowly back to the rest of the team and took his place at the end of the bench. When he sat down, he leaned over and covered his face with his hands.

"Don't worry," I called over to him. "We're three runs ahead. Besides, in a minute I'm going to hit everyone home."

Tony's dad had been standing away from the bench, but now he walked over and stood in front of Tony. "What happened out there?"

Tony shook his head. "I don't know."

But I knew. Tony was too busy concentrating on the competition going on in the bleachers to think about the competition here on the field.

"We can't afford to give outs away," Coach said. Then he looked at me. "Come on, McKay, you're up after Johnson."

I walked out to the field, picked up my bat, and swung it in practice a few times. This hit had to be great. This hit would be for Tony, so his dad would stop thinking about his strikeout.

Johnson hit a blooper to left field, then jogged to first base. With his face still red from the run, he took a one-step lead off the base and stood paused, watching me.

I stepped up to the plate and focused on the pitcher. He pulled back and threw. I swung and hit. I could tell from the sound of the ball hitting the wood, from the sting of the ball against my bat, that the hit was a good one. The ball soared past the outfielders and bounced down in far left field. I sprinted around the bases, with each breath forcing myself to go faster. It looked like it was going to be close when I came around third base. One of the infielders had the ball and was throwing it in. Still, I pushed on and with one last surge of energy, slid into home plate. I felt a glove come down on my side, but only after I'd grabbed onto the plate. I was safe, and a moment later the umpire gave the safe sign.

I stood up, brushed myself off, then walked, breathless, back to the bench. The team all hollered and gave me high fives. Tony gave me two.

The rest of the game went by quickly. When it was over, we'd won by five runs. It was a great feeling to walk off the field.

All three girls came over to congratulate us.

"Great game," Serena told me.

"I'm glad I came to see it," Rachel said, and she glared at Tony.

"Uh, thanks," Tony said. He looked from Rachel to Anna and back.

Anna didn't say anything, but she blushed.

"Well, we'd better go now," Serena said, and before anyone else could say anything, she and Rachel walked off.

Anna said, "I'd better go too," but she went in a different direction.

Tony watched her for a moment then said, "Man, that was uncomfortable. I guess I should have checked to see whether Rachel was coming before I invited Anna to watch the game."

"You invited her?" I grabbed Tony's baseball cap off his head and leaned toward him as if I was examining him. "Stand still, I'm checking to see if you have any brain cells left."

Tony grabbed the hat back from me and put it on his head. "I invited her because she likes baseball."

"Oh, sure, just like Jenna does."

We walked slowly to the crowd that had dispersed around the bleachers. Tony said, "Actually, it's over between Jenna and Adam."

"Did he find her out?"

"No, she finally came to the conclusion he could never love her as much as he loves Babe Ruth. She decided she no longer wanted to take the backseat to a dead baseball player."

My family found me then, and I got congratulated some more. My dad said, "I knew you could pull it off." My mom said, "You played great." Kirk said, "We won! We won! We won!"

"That's right," I told him. "And I didn't have to trip anyone."

"Yeah," he said, "but you might want to try that next time."

The next day Serena materialized at my locker as I was getting ready for first period. I said, "Oh, hi Serena," and held my locker door as close to being shut as I could without smashing parts of my body inside. Every time Serena came by my locker, I vowed

I'd straighten it up so I wouldn't have to be embarrassed about it next time, but I always forgot.

"Hi, McKay." She leaned against the next locker without showing the slightest interest in the disorderly state of mine. She also didn't seem to notice the odd way I took my books out of the small slit of an opening I'd created by closing my locker most of the way.

Serena handed me a note and in a somber voice said, "It's for Tony. Rachel is breaking up with him. You might want to, you know, sort of prepare him for the news."

"Oh, uh, yeah." Exactly how did she imagine I was supposed to prepare him? And besides, if the last few days of note passing hadn't prepared him for trouble, certainly nothing I could say would. I was just glad this was the last note I had to play postman with.

Then a terrible thought occurred to me. If Serena didn't have any notes for me to deliver, maybe she wouldn't stop by my locker anymore. Or worse yet, maybe because of all of this fighting with Tony, she wouldn't want anything to do with me. This was a bad thought. As I pulled out my English book, I said, "We're still studying after school at my house, right?"

"Sure." She brushed a strand of long brown hair back into place. "Well I'd better get to class." She turned to go, but before she left said, "Let me know how Tony takes the news."

I walked to English and wondered if all girls gave such impossible requests. She wanted me to let her know how Tony took the news? If Tony didn't care, and I told Serena that, it would cement both Rachel's and Serena's dislike for him. If Tony was all broken up about it, and I told Serena that, Tony would be so embarrassed he'd pound some of my internal organs out of shape, and I'd have to let him, because I'd deserve it. You just didn't give out that sort of information about your best friend. So really the only solution to this problem was for me to either avoid the subject altogether, or make up something that wouldn't enrage the girls or mortify Tony. Only I didn't know what that was.

This is where having an older brother to confer with would have come in handy, but I was older-brotherless. Kirk was the lucky one. By the time he got to junior high, I'd have girls all figured out and be able to tell him what to say in any situation. Kirk would probably be so cool he wouldn't even have to practice a walk. Coolness would just be second nature to him.

I trudged down the hall to my first class and hoped I'd have some inspiration before I talked to Serena again.

I didn't see Tony until we were heading to algebra class. I handed him the note. "Here," I said. It was the best I could do to prepare him.

He read the note then crumpled it up and threw it into one of the hallway trash cans. "Rachel broke up with me." He didn't sound very concerned about this turn of events.

"Oh?" I asked. "And what exactly is your reaction to that?"

He shrugged. "In some ways it makes things easier. I was a little afraid that if I broke up with Rachel and then asked Anna out, it might make me look, you know, mean or something. But since Rachel broke up with me, it's not mean of me to ask out her friend."

Nope, this was definitely not something I'd tell Serena about. I could just imagine what her reaction would be if I reported back to her exactly how Tony took the news.

Me: He was grateful Rachel broke up with him, because now he can ask Anna out without looking mean.

Serena (with a shocked expression, because it is suddenly clear to her that Tony and Rachel were never even remotely close to Romeo and Juliet): He what?

Me: Yeah, and then he started humming as we walked to algebra class.

I'd just have to think of something else to tell Serena. "After he got the news, he was very thoughtful," I'd tell her, because after all, Tony must have been thinking about something as he walked humming down the hall.

Serena never asked me how he took the news, though. By the time school was over, Tony and Anna were walking around in the halls together, so I guess it was apparent to everyone he didn't take the news very hard. While we were walking to my house, Serena told me she wasn't exactly mad at Tony and Anna, she was just extremely *disappointed,* and she had *nothing* else to say about them. This was fine with me. I didn't want to talk about them either. I asked her about horses, and she told me about some horseback riding trips she'd taken with her family in the Superstition Mountains. "Have you ever been there?" she asked.

The Superstition Mountains were about a half-hour drive from our house. Dad and I hiked up them at least once a year. I knew Serena was specifically asking if I'd ever done them on a horse, but I decided to ignore this fact and answered, "Sure. They're great." I'd been purposefully vague about my horse experience since our first conversation.

When we got to my house, the first thing I did after we walked in the door was to call, "Mom, we're home."

After a moment Mom appeared in the hallway. "Hi, kids. There are some snacks in the kitchen. I'm right in the middle of Dr. Nebonski's chest X-ray diagnosis, so I'll be in the office." She went back down the hall, and I had to stifle the urge to call after her, "Hey, Mom, come back here. You haven't had a chance yet to notice how polite Serena is."

Instead I set my stuff down on the couch. Mom would be back later. I was sure of it. I was sure because I'd suddenly noticed how clean the house was. Mom never cleaned the house when Tony came over. She'd be back.

Serena sat down on the couch and pulled her algebra book from her backpack. While she was arranging her notes, I went into the kitchen and put some popcorn in the microwave.

I'd just got a couple of bowls down from the cupboard when I heard Kirk come into the family room.

"Hi. You must be Kirk," I heard Serena say.

"Are you going to marry my brother?" he answered.

I popped back into the family room. "Go away, Kirk, and don't bug us. We're trying to study."

He said, "You're not studying, you're eating."

"You still have to go away."

He picked up my algebra notebook. "I just want some paper to make airplanes."

Before he could rip out any of my assignments, I rushed over and grabbed the notebook away from him. "Find your own paper. I'm using this."

He stood planted to the ground and gave me his stubborn stare. I returned his stare with my move-right-now-or-I'll-hurt-you stare. He still didn't move, so I said, "Do you want me to tell Mom you're bothering us while we're trying to study?"

He turned and stomped off in the direction of our bedroom.

I glanced over at Serena to see if she was upset at having her marriage plans questioned, but she was just smirking and looked like she was trying hard not to laugh.

"Sorry about that," I said.

"It's okay. I think he's cute."

Most people think Kirk is cute. None of these people have to live with him, though.

I went back into the kitchen and brought out the popcorn. A few pieces of it had burned because, instead of watching it, I had been banishing Kirk from the family room. I hoped Serena didn't mind too much.

We decided the best way to study for the test would be to go over questions from each of the assignments to make sure we still remembered how to work them. We were about halfway through with this when Kirk made his next appearance. He had a half a dozen paper airplanes and took them with him behind the love seat in the family room.

"What are you doing in here, Kirk?" I asked him. "You're not supposed to bother us."

Kirk didn't answer. He just made jet noises and launched one of his airplanes toward us. I caught it midair. "Kaboom," I said. "Your plane has been shot down." Without even looking at it, I wadded it up and tossed it back at the love seat. "Now go play somewhere else."

Kirk poked his head over the love seat. Making even bigger jet noises, he threw two more airplanes toward us. I caught one, crumpled it up, and hurled it back at Kirk, but the other landed by Serena, and she picked it up gingerly.

"Come on," I told her, "show me your best pitching form."

Instead of crumpling it up, she unfolded the plane. "What is this?"

I hadn't even bothered looking at the airplanes, but now as she uncreased the paper I recognized my handwriting. "Ohhh," she said in a teasing voice, "A note from Tony."

At first I thought she was joking. How could Kirk have gotten a note from Tony to make into a paper airplane? Then it hit me with a terrible thud of realization. I'd taken notes out of my math folder and put them in my dresser—my dresser that Kirk thought he could dig through whenever he pleased. I reached for the paper, but Serena held it away from me. "Oh no, you don't. It's about me, and it's just getting good."

The thud of realization suddenly grew into a feeling very similar to being run down by a large truck. I didn't remember what I'd ever written about Serena, but whatever it was, I didn't want her to see it. I lunged for the note again, but she jumped off the couch.

"Give me that note," I told her.

She held onto the paper and read out loud, "I've noticed she and Rachel giggle a lot when I walk by now." She looked up from the paper at me. "We do not."

"Give me that paper," I said in the most serious voice I could manage.

Serena went on reading out loud, "She must like you. You must like her."

I lunged for the paper again. This time I got it, but I could tell from the look on her face she'd read the next part anyway. Her expression was a cross between wanting to cry and wanting to hit me.

"You don't like me?" she asked, but it wasn't really a question. "You just wanted me to help you in math?"

"No—I mean, well, I wanted you to help me with math, but I didn't mean, I mean—" I didn't know what I meant, but she didn't give me time to explain anyway. She picked up her books from the couch and shoved them into her backpack.

"I didn't mean that I didn't like you," I said weakly.

"Then why did you write it?" She flung her backpack onto her shoulder.

I hadn't thought about that note since I wrote it. Under the spotlight of the moment, I didn't remember what exactly had been going on or why I had worded things that way. "I don't know," I said. I looked down and saw the words I'd written on the note, *I don't like her. I just want her to help me with my math.* "I'm sorry, Serena."

By this time Serena was walking to my front door. "Oh, give me a break, McKay. You were just using me to help you get a better grade in math, and you know it." She swung the front door open, but paused before she stepped outside. "And you know what else, suddenly I understand why you're best friends with Tony Manetti." She slammed the door as she left.

I thought about going after her and trying to explain things, trying to apologize again. But what could I say to fix this? I stared at the front door and wished I could kick it. This was not just a little social blunder. It was an earthquake. How did a guy go about trying to put things back together after an earthquake?

I needed time to come up with a really good apology. Or I at least needed enough time that Serena would cool off and accept a partially good apology. And I wasn't even sure I could come up with that. At this point I was only sure of one thing, and that was that Kirk was responsible for this earthquake, and therefore should suffer for it.

I walked back into the family room to face him. He was still standing behind the love seat with a paper plane grasped in his hand. He had no idea what had just happened, and I could tell he wasn't exactly sure whether he was in trouble or not. I sent him an angry glare to clear up the matter in his little mind. "I'll kill you," I said, "slowly and painfully."

He yelled, "Mom!" and took off toward the back of the house. I didn't chase after him. Instead I went up to our room and started putting all of Kirk's things out in the hallway. I'd cleared out all of his guns, swords, and Star Wars figures before Mom walked in. She had one hand on her hip, and one hand holding onto Kirk's hand. He stood as far away from me as he could and sniffled.

"Did you tell your brother you'd tear his legs off?" she asked

"No, but if I had thought of it, I would have."

"See! See!" Kirk pointed at me wildly. "I told you he was going to hurt me."

"He's not going to hurt you," Mom said sternly.

"Yes I am," I said, "because he's ruining my life." I walked over to my dresser, opened the top drawer, and pointed at the now empty space that my notes used to be in. "He got into my stuff and made paper airplanes out of my personal, private notes. He threw one I'd written about Serena to her, and she read it. Now she's mad at me, and it's all Kirk's fault."

Mom looked down at Kirk. "Oh, Kirk, you didn't, did you?"

Kirk had three of his fingers in his mouth—half sucking on them, half biting down. He's done this ever since he was a baby whenever he gets nervous or scared.

Mom said, "You know you're not allowed to get into McKay's things."

Kirk bit on his fingers some more and didn't say anything.

Usually when I see Kirk like this, I start to feel sorry for him. But not this time. I picked his cowboy boots out of the closet and dropped them into the hallway.

Mom said, "What are you doing, McKay?"

"Moving Kirk out of this room and away from my stuff."

I thought Mom would protest. I thought she'd order me to put all of Kirk's stuff back. In fact, I'd already prepared my arguments against doing it. But Mom didn't stop me. She just looked down at Kirk sympathetically and sighed. "I guess it really is about time for the two of you to have separate rooms. Then maybe you won't be at each other's throats all of the time."

"What?" Kirk wailed, and then, "but this is my room too!" Then he stomped his feet up and down.

Mom's look of sympathy disappeared. She hated it when Kirk threw temper tantrums. "Come on. You can help me get the office ready for your things."

"No!" Kirk wailed even louder. "Make McKay put my stuff back! Make him!"

Mom pulled Kirk out of the room and down the hallway. I could hear him screaming all the way there.

I kept moving things into the hallway. With every coloring book and Pokémon card I dropped into the pile, I was closer to freedom. By dinnertime I had all of Kirk's things out of the room.

I studied for the test, silently, sprawled across my bed. I knew how to do all of the practice problems. This was a relief, but I couldn't bring myself to be happy about it. I couldn't feel happy about anything. At eight o'clock I called Serena's house. Her mother said she was still at the mall. I didn't bother to ask her to call me back. I knew she wouldn't.

The next day at school I tried to find Serena in the hall, but the one time I saw her, she was with Brian Vanders. They were standing together outside algebra class, and she was smiling up at him. She looked at me for a second when I walked past, then returned her gaze to Brian and laughed at something he'd said.

It was hard to concentrate on the algebra test. I read off the first problem to myself: $4x - y = 2 - 2(y/2 - x)$. I got halfway through working out the equation, then glanced across the room at Serena to see what she was doing. She was writing with a serious look on her face. I finished the problem then went to the next, $x^2 + 7x = -12$. I glanced over at Serena again. Did she really like Brian? If so, were they going to hang out together outside algebra class every day? The thought made my intestines feel like they were having a tug of war.

I read the last question. If this and that and blah blah blah, when would two trains meet in Boston? If only all of my problems could be answered so easily.

After I finished the test, I stared at my desk. I tried to recheck some of the harder problems on the test, but the numbers didn't seem to mean anything. I peered over at Serena for a while longer. She'd finished her test too and was brushing off some eraser marks from one corner of her paper.

Look at me, I told her silently. Just glance over here so I know you're thinking about me.

She put her test squarely in the middle of her desk and turned her attention to the clock hanging on the wall.

She'd probably ignore me forever. I wondered if every algebra class from here on would be this way. It almost sounded like a story problem. If McKay looks over at Serena at a rate of once every 2 minutes, and class lasts for 55 minutes every day, how long will it take before he goes absolutely insane? I knew I had to talk to her. I couldn't go through this intestine-stretching experience every day. I had to find a way to explain to her that the note to Tony didn't mean anything. It happened before I got to know her. It was just talk. It was because Tony was blowing kisses at me and picking out names for our firstborn son. The problem was, I didn't know how to tell her any of that.

I looked down at the pencil in my hand. Maybe it would be best to write it down in a note. That way I could make sure I said everything exactly the way I should. But then the more I thought about it, the more I thought a note was a bad idea. Maybe Serena would show it to Brian, and they'd both laugh about what a loser I was. Maybe Serena would make it into a paper airplane and throw it back at me.

Tony walked with me to my locker after class. "How did you do on the test?" he asked me.

"I think I did pretty well."

"Me too," he said. "What time did your trains meet in Boston?"

"Five-thirty."

"Dang. Mine met at four-twelve."

I opened my locker and got my sack lunch out.

"Hey, I forgot to tell you," Tony said. "I'm going out with Anna now."

"Great." I slammed my locker door shut.

"But I found out some bad news for you. Anna told me Serena and Brian are going out now."

"Really?" My intestines began an Olympic version of a tug-of-war.

"Yeah. He asked her this morning. Lousy break, huh?"

"Yeah. Lousy break."

"But there are a lot of other cute girls around. You've just got to get out there and start playing the field if you want to win the game."

I didn't answer him. I didn't know what to say. The last thing I wanted to do at this moment was to start chasing another girl. My insides hadn't recovered from the last one.

That afternoon we played the South Mesa Toros for game four. I was especially glad when I got to the ballpark. I knew once I stepped onto the field, I wouldn't think about anything except the game. And I didn't think about Serena at all—well, except for the few times I glanced at the bleachers and noticed she wasn't there watching me play.

I hit a beautiful triple in the first inning. We won 8 to 5, which meant we only had three more teams to beat, and we'd win the district fall ball title. Our team was jazzed. As we got ready to go home, all the guys on the team did a lot of yelling and backslapping. Tony and I did several verses of our "You the man" song. I felt great. I was the man of all men.

The next day at school I was no longer McKay the man. I was McKay the guy who'd messed up with Serena, and not only was she still giving me the major cold shoulder, but I noticed Rachel threw some icicle looks at me too. She turned away sharply from me whenever I walked by her in the hallway. I wondered who else knew about my note to Tony and was also mad at me. And how long did girls stay mad once they got that way? Thinking about all of this made me yearn for the good old days when I was flunking math.

At the end of algebra class, Mrs. Swenson handed our tests back. I got an 86, which was a B+. It was the best grade I'd received on a test all year. She actually congratulated me as she handed it to me.

My parents would be thrilled about this. I watched Serena tuck her test into her algebra book and leave the room without even a glance in my direction. Somehow my B+ didn't seem as great without being able to tell her about it.

I thought about this all the way home, and off and on for the rest of the night. I tried to call Serena after dinner, but I got the answering machine. I wondered if she had caller ID and just wasn't answering the phone because she knew it was me. I hung up without leaving a message.

When I woke up the next morning, I still had a sinking feeling every time I thought about Serena. I knew I had to talk to her soon. I was going to offer a real apology, and Serena was going to listen to me. Then, if she still wanted to be mad at me—well, fine, she could be mad, but it wouldn't be because I hadn't done my part to try and patch things up.

The only problem with this plan was that it was Saturday, and I wouldn't be able to go to school and see her. This was probably the first day in my entire school career I woke up and wished the weekend was over. I stewed around all morning while I did my chores and thought of the things I ought to say to Serena and how I should word everything to best defend myself. By the afternoon I had quite a speech worked out. I was half afraid I'd forget it by Monday, or at least that I'd lose my nerve and not be able to talk to Serena at school. So I did a very brave thing. After I'd finished the last of the vacuuming, I got on my bike and rode over to Serena's house.

I stood on her porch for a few moments and went over bits and pieces of my speech. I wondered if Serena would answer the door or whether it would be her mother. I really hoped it wouldn't be her father. I'd never met him, and I was a little afraid he'd be the overly protective type who didn't like boys visiting his daughter. Maybe Serena had told her parents all about the note incident, and now neither one of them liked me, and they'd scowl when they saw me standing at their door. Finally I rang the bell.

Serena's mother answered the door with a smile. "Oh, hello, McKay. Serena's already left."

"Oh," I said blankly. "Left?" I had been so prepared to offer some sort of defense on the doorstep that I just stood there looking at Mrs. Kimball, not sure what to do next.

When I didn't leave right away, Mrs. Kimball said, "I'm sure you could catch up with her. She's right down the street."

She seemed to think I ought to know what she was talking about, and I didn't want to admit I didn't. "Oh," I said again, and then, "Well, thanks." I got back on my bike and for the first time noticed a bunch of kids down the street on bikes. I couldn't tell who they were from a distance, but I slowly rode my bike in their direction anyway.

I hadn't planned to give my speech in front of anyone but Serena, and when I gave it to her, she was supposed to be giving me her full attention. She was also supposed to have a sort of wistful look about her that would let me know that she too was sorry we'd ever had this fight. I didn't want to talk to her while she was with a group. I pedaled my bike a little slower. Maybe my speech could wait until Monday.

Then again, I was already here. I didn't want to turn around and go home now. I might as well go down there and see what Serena was doing. I could just pretend I was in this part of the neighborhood and casually go by. Then if Serena wasn't busy, or surrounded by a lot of people or something, I might stop and say hi.

When I got closer, I saw what was going on. The group of kids, which consisted mostly of half a dozen guys from our school, had turned a couple of empty lots into a bike jumping course. They'd built up some mounds of dirt and were riding their bikes over them. The lowest mound was probably only a foot and a half off the ground and the highest was three, so they didn't look dangerous or spectacular, but the guys made a big deal about it anyway, whooping it up as they went over.

Personally speaking, Tony and I had gone over bigger jumps back when we were ten years old, going through our stuntman phase. For a full year Tony and I were determined that one day we'd go to Hollywood and become professional stuntmen. We figured it would be best to get an early start on learning stunt-man skills, so we'd jumped our bikes, leaped off Tony's deck, practiced falling down the stairs, and worked on an assortment of other stuntmanlike activities. My mom finally put an end to our Hollywood ambitions when she caught us lighting newspapers in the street so we could run through them. I was grounded for a month and had to live with the threat that if I ever, ever tried to be a stuntman again, Mom would lock me in my room until I was old enough to pay for my own medical insurance.

So anyway, I was not overly impressed by this bike jump course, or with the jumpers, especially since one of them was Brian Vanders. I stopped in the street a little way from every-body and watched them for a minute. I saw Rachel standing by one of the boys, talking with him, but I didn't see Serena at first. Then I noticed her sitting on a half wall at the back of the lot. She had probably originally been watching Brian do jumps, but now she was watching me. She gave me a long look, not smiling but not glaring either. It was just a long look, then she turned her attention back to the group of boys.

Tony, I suppose, would have known exactly what that look meant and whether it would have been better to stop now and try to make amends with Serena or whether that look meant it was better to stay on my bike and keep going. But I wasn't Tony, and I didn't know. I figured since she'd seen me, I'd better stop and talk to her. I didn't have to issue my apology right now. I'd just say hi and be friendly, then I'd leave.

I rode my bike up to where Serena sat but didn't get off.

"Hi, Serena."

She glanced at me, but only briefly. "Hi."

I took a deep breath and tried to look casual. "How did you do on your algebra test?"

"I got an A."

I waited for her to ask how I'd done, but she didn't, so I said, "I got a B+."

"Good. I guess you got all you wanted then."

I cleared my throat. "You know that's not all I wanted. I mean, of course I wanted to raise my math grade and everything, but, well, you know what I mean."

Serena raised her eyebrows at me. "No, I don't know what you mean."

"I mean that I never meant what I said in that note to Tony."

"Oh, really? Then you must have written that stuff because you were practicing your handwriting skills, right?" Her eyebrows were still raised.

"No, Tony was giving me a hard time about you, you know, so I just . . ." I tapped my handlebars nervously. This was not at all what I'd planned on saying. "I never meant I didn't like you. I just meant I didn't like you, like picking-out-names like you, and besides, that was before I even knew you, you know?"

She looked straight at me and said, "McKay, most of the time you make absolutely no sense."

Just then Brian rode up to us. He looked me over suspiciously, then turned and smiled at Serena. "Did you see that last jump?"

"Yeah." Serena beamed back at him. "It was great."

"I was airborne for probably five seconds." He took a deep breath as though just thinking about this great accomplishment took a vast amount of energy.

Serena still smiled adoringly at him. "That must be really hard."

"You just have to be in good shape." He looked scornfully over at me. "It's a lot harder than hitting a baseball around."

"Like you'd know," I said back to him.

"Hey, if you think jumping is so easy, then why don't you try it?" Brian said.

"I have tried it."

"Then show us," he said.

I glanced over at Serena to see what she thought of Brian's challenging me like this, but I couldn't tell what was going on in her mind. She was just watching me, waiting to see what I'd do next.

"All right," I said. "I'll jump one of your stupid little mounds."

Somewhere in the back of my mind, I heard a voice, probably Coach Manetti's voice, telling me this was a foolish thing to do, but I didn't listen. A guy didn't walk away from a challenge like this, at least not while Serena Kimball sat there watching. Besides, I could make the jump. I knew I could.

I rode my bike over to one of the mid-size mounds and got in line behind a couple of other guys. They hadn't heard Brian's challenge to me, but they didn't seem surprised I'd joined in their line anyway.

"Hey, McKay, you gonna jump?" one of the guys asked me.

"Sure. I thought I'd give it a shot."

Brian was still over by Serena, watching me. I guess he'd decided he'd better stick by his girlfriend in case anyone else tried to muscle in on her attention.

The guy in front of me went over the mound. He skidded a bit on landing, but all in all made a successful jump.

So now it was my turn. I took a deep breath, checked to make sure my bike helmet was in position, then took off toward the mound. There was one small moment, when I was in the air and felt myself coming down, that I felt a bubble of panic in my chest. But it only lasted a moment. Then I was on the ground and steering my bike back toward Serena and Brian. "See," I shrugged. "Nothing to it."

"Well, sure, you went over the smallest jump," Brian said—out-and-out lying, I might add. "Any fourth-grader could go over that one. Why don't you try the big one?" Then he pointed in the direction of the three-foot mound.

"Okay," I said. "Right after you."

"No problem." Brian got back on his bike and pedaled over to the big mound. I followed a little way behind him. He only paused for a moment in front of the mound, then got up his speed and went over. He was in the air for probably three seconds, then his bike thumped back ȯnto the ground. It wobbled for a second, but he straightened it up and rode back toward me. "Your turn now."

"No problem," I called back to him. I positioned my bike in front of the mound. And you know, it's funny, but as I sat there surveying it, the mound suddenly looked a lot bigger than it had before. I pedaled toward it and scolded myself for being nervous. If Brian could manage to jump it, then so could I. Then we'd see whether Brian was still gloating. I'd ride right back to him and Serena and say, "See, jumping your silly little mounds is tons easier than hitting a baseball. Hitting a baseball takes talent. Any idiot can ride his bike over a pile of dirt."

And that's when I rode mine over. At the top of the mound I lifted the front wheel of my bike and flew through the air. It was a beautiful thing. It was how the baseball must feel as it's soaring toward the outfield fence. And then I touched the ground. Literally. My bike landed, and for a second I thought I was going to be okay, but only for a second. My front tire skidded across the dirt. My back tire spun around like it was trying to get in front of me, and then suddenly I was on the ground with my bike on top of me.

I'm sure it was a spectacular crash to all those who were watching—which, unfortunately, was everybody.

I don't know what was worse, the pain that shot through my entire body, or knowing I'd just made a complete fool of myself in front of Brian and Serena. I lay on the ground for a moment to get my breath back. Before I was able to sit up, a couple of the guys came and hovered over me.

"Are you all right, McKay?" one of them said.

"Oh sure," I said. "I'm just lying here admiring the dirt." I sat up slowly and pushed my bike off of me.

"Cool crash," the other kid said.

I stared back at him. "Yeah, cool." He'd obviously been in one too many bike wrecks himself, and his brain had stopped working.

I tried to ignore the sharp pains throbbing in my foot and leg as I stood up. I brushed dirt off my pants and shirt, and was glad to see I didn't have blood gushing from anywhere.

At this point Serena and Brian came and hovered around with everyone else. She looked concerned. He looked smug.

"Are you okay?" she asked.

"Yeah, I'm fine."

"Your bike doesn't look so good though." Brian picked up my bike. Instead of pointing forward, the front wheel was bent sideways.

"Too bad," I said, "or I could try that jump again. I'd have been able to land right if I'd timed my lift better." I knew I couldn't even walk, let alone try another bike stunt, but I wasn't going to let Brian know this. I would have hopped one-legged all the way home rather than ask him for help.

"You almost made it," Serena said. I knew she felt sorry for me.

I bent over my bike and tried to bend the wheel straight. Serena must have noticed I was keeping all of my weight off my left leg because she looked down at it and said, "Are you sure you're all right, McKay?"

"I'm fine." I had no idea how I'd make it home. Even if I hadn't just pretzelized my bike, I doubt I could have ridden it. I tried to imagine myself limping down the street while simultaneously dragging my bike behind me. I fiddled with the front wheel, trying to straighten it out because I didn't know what else to do.

"I don't think you'll be able to fix it," Serena said. "And you also have a nasty scrape on your chin, McKay. Do you want to call your parents to come and get you?"

I put my hand on my chin. With all of the other pain throbbing around in my body, I hadn't even noticed my chin. Now it began to sting, and when I took my hand away there was blood on it. Great. Not only had I wrecked my bike, and in all probability broken my leg, I was now disfigured to boot. Things just kept getting better and better.

Serena didn't wait for me to answer. She turned and said, "I'll go call them." She was a few feet away before I realized I hadn't given her my phone number.

"Hey, Serena," I yelled after her. "You don't know my number."

She only turned to me for a moment. "Yes, I do," she yelled back, and then kept walking toward her house.

I returned to the task of fiddling with my front tire so I wouldn't have to say anything to the other guys. They had already moved their bikes to another mound and were now cheering each other on to perform more acts of daring and stupidity. Brian was about to do another jump, this time only using one hand to hold onto his handlebars.

"Hey, McKay," he shouted over at me. "Watch and learn from a pro!"

I hoped he'd skid and fall and his bike would spontaneously explode when it hit the ground, but none of these things happened. It was a perfectly smooth jump.

Serena and her mom pulled up in their minivan and stopped a little way from me. Mrs. Kimball got out and said, "I thought I'd better take you home instead of waiting for your parents to come, just in case you're seriously hurt." Then she put my bike in the back of the minivan.

"Thanks." I staggered into the van after her. I didn't even care that it was Serena's mom who was taking me home. At this point, I had no pride left.

The whole way to my house, my leg throbbed. All I could think was, This injury is not going to go away anytime soon, and I'll most likely miss our last three games. Coach Manetti was going to kill me. That was, if I didn't kill myself first. How could I have done something so foolish? Right at the end of the tournament was not the time to think I could take on Brian Vander's ego, my mortality, or the law of gravity. What had I been thinking? Well, I knew what I'd been thinking. I'd been thinking about Serena, and I was going to stop thinking about her right now. Girls. Who needed them? They were nothing but trouble in eyeshadow. I refused to even look at Serena for the entire ride.

When we pulled up to my house, I mumbled a thanks to Serena's mom. She offered to help me inside the house, but I said I could manage, so she just unloaded my bike while I dragged myself to the door.

Mom, to say the least, was surprised to see me in this condition. She didn't even bother changing out of her Saturday cleaning clothes. She just put hydrogen peroxide on my chin and then drove me to the urgent care clinic.

We had to sit in the waiting room for a long time, so Kirk tried to make me feel better by reading me stories. Mom always read stories to him when he was sick, so he was certain it would make me feel better too. He couldn't actually find any books, so he picked up a magazine and opened it to the first page. It was a car advertisement. He said, "Once there was a family who went for a ride." He turned the next page and saw an ad for soap. "They got dirty, so then they had to go take baths." On the next page was a picture of a Timex. "Even their watches got baths," he said, then looked up at me. "Do you feel better yet?"

"Yeah."

"You're still bleeding," he said. "I'd better read to you some more."

He went through the whole magazine that way. The family in the story didn't actually do anything, but they saw a lot of interesting stuff and took lots of car rides.

◇

I finally got to see a doctor. He poked and prodded my leg and ankle—I apparently wasn't in enough pain to begin with— then sent me for X rays.

After the X rays were completed, I went back into the doctor's office with Mom and Kirk to wait for the results. A few minutes later he came back.

"You're a lucky young man," he said as he sat down. "It's only a sprained ankle." Then he lectured me about the dangers of jumping bikes and how I could have easily broken bones, gotten a concussion, or something worse. He waved his pen at me and said, "So I don't ever want you to jump a bike again. You might not be so lucky next time."

"When will I be able to play baseball again?" I asked.

"You won't be able to run on that leg for a couple of weeks," he said.

So really, when you came down to it, I wasn't that lucky after all. I slumped down in my seat. I didn't hear anything else the doctor had to say. He gave Mom instructions of some sort, but I didn't listen. Why should I? The next three games would decide the district title, and I wouldn't be able to play in any of them. I was going to miss everything I'd been working for during the last season. I'd let my team down, and I'd let myself down. Life, basically, was worthless.

I only remember one other thing that happened at the doctor's visit. While I sat there and tried not to humiliate myself by doing something like crying in front of the medical staff, Kirk knelt down and surveyed my leg. After a moment he leaned over and gave it a quick kiss. Then he stood up and whispered in my ear, "I kissed it all better so you'll be able to play baseball again."

Once I got home, I lay on the couch with ice packs on my leg and sulked. What I wanted was a miracle. I wanted all of the swelling in my ankle to suddenly go down, the pain to go away, and for it to not look purple and green anymore. I wanted to get up off the couch and practice ball with Kirk in the backyard. One lousy miracle was all I was asking for.

I thought about calling Tony so I could have someone to complain to, but I didn't dare. I didn't want to have to talk to Coach Manetti. I dreaded telling him the McKay Cannon had been defused. I dreaded hearing what he'd say. It was easier to lie on the couch and hope for a miracle.

As it turned out, my mom made the call to Coach. While I was still on the couch feeling sorry for myself, I heard her in the kitchen explaining the situation to him. After she'd told him the news, a few moments of silence followed, and then she said, "Mmmhmm," and "We'll see," and then "I'll tell him."

She came back into the family room, and I said, "You'll tell me what?" It probably had something to do with the coach wanting to break my other leg.

"Mr. Manetti said to tell you he's sorry you got hurt, and he hopes you feel better soon."

I guess coaches don't tell mothers what they're really thinking.

"He says if you're feeling up to it during any of the games, you can still bat and have someone run for you."

My outlook immediately brightened. I could still bat, couldn't I? I had forgotten that was allowed. As long as I could run to first base, I could have a pinch runner go the rest of the way for me. That might be impossible for the next game—it was only a few days away—but the other two games, surely by then I'd be well enough to stagger to first base. "I'll feel up to it," I said, and pulled myself up a little on the couch to prove the point.

Mom looked at me skeptically. "Let's not rush anything. We'll see how you're doing at game time."

Mom walked out of the room, and Kirk walked in. He carried a plate and very proudly set it down beside me. "Here, I made you a sandwich to help you feel better."

"Thanks." I picked up the sandwich and looked it over suspiciously. Kirk has never caught onto the fact that not all sandwich contents go together, and he has a habit of making all sorts of peculiar combinations. Then he actually eats them. Things that would make any normal person gag, Kirk wolfs down with glee. I've even caught him eating spoonfuls of mayonnaise from the jar. "So what kind of sandwich is it?" I asked.

"Peanut butter and mustard."

"Oh."

He watched me expectantly, waiting for me to take a bite. And really, what could I do? When I thought of him on the countertop by himself making a sandwich for me, I knew I had to at least choke down some of it. I took a bite and chewed it quickly. "Mmm. Thanks, Kirk." It could have been worse, I suppose. It could have been a peanut butter and jelly and mustard sandwich.

"I'm glad you're my brother," I told him, and I meant it. It was nice to know that no matter what kind of stupid things I did in life, Kirk would be there for me. Even if being there only meant he read me stories in the emergency room and then made me sandwiches. He was my brother, and that would never change. "You're a pretty cool guy," I added.

"I know," he said.

I put the sandwich back on the plate. "I feel kind of bad making you move into the office."

He sat up straighter. "You want to share our room again?"

"Well, not exactly. I just thought I'd let you keep the old room, and I'll move into the office. Then every once in a while I'll come back and visit you."

He still smiled over this bit of news. "Can I have the baseball posters too?"

I shrugged. "Yeah, I guess I can get some new ones for my room."

He jumped up and gave me a hug. He landed a little on my leg, which I'm sure did nothing to help my recovery, but I didn't complain. Then he got down and said, "I'm going to tell Mom I get my room back." I guess he figured he'd better go make the decision official before I changed my mind.

A few minutes later the doorbell rang, but I didn't pay any attention to it. I was busy wiggling my toes to see if they hurt less now than right after the accident. I was hoping for an improvement. Any improvement.

Mom came into the family room with Serena behind her.

"You have a visitor," Mom said.

I stopped wiggling my toes. "Uh, hi."

Serena looked at my leg propped up on the pillows and the ice pack on my ankle. "How bad is it?"

"It's only a sprain," I said, and then added for Mom's sake, "And it's feeling a lot better already."

"I'm glad to hear that," Serena said. "I was worried about you."

I shrugged in what I hoped was a macho cavalier manner. "It was just a little crash. I've been in worse." Right after I said it, I realized this sounded more stupid than macho. Mom was pursing her lips together, probably in an attempt not to laugh. I guess this was for the best though, otherwise she might enforce her threat to make me pay for my medical insurance. I tried to think of something better to say, but didn't come up with anything.

"Well, I'm glad you're all right," Serena said. She'd been hiding one hand behind her back, and now she brought out a bouquet of yellow lantana and held it out to me. "These are for you. I picked them myself."

I took them from her, and a few of the blossoms fell onto my lap.

"Gee. Thanks. No card?"

"I couldn't get past 'Dear McKay.'"

Mom looked back and forth between Serena and me like she couldn't quite decide what to make of us or the bouquet.

I held the flowers out to her. "Uh, Mom, can you put these in water for me?"

"Sure." Mom took the bouquet but held it a little ways away from her. She walked out of the family room, leaving a trail of little yellow blossoms as she went.

Serena sat down on our old gray recliner by the couch, and we stared at each other for a moment.

"I'm sorry about that note to Tony," I told her. "It really didn't mean anything. It was just stupid guy talk."

"I'm not mad about it anymore. It's hard to be mad at you when you're hurt. And I know the only reason you even did that jump was because you wanted to talk to me." She shrugged, and a section of her hair slid from her shoulders. "I know Brian was a real jerk to you. I talked to him about it after we took you home." She tilted her head at me. "It's funny, but I started off the day angry at you, and now I'm angry at him."

"You're angry at Brian now?"

She looked up at me and said softly, "Yeah." It wasn't really an answer. It was a question—she wanted some indication of how I felt about her. Only now that she was going out with Brian, it didn't seem right that I say anything at all about her and me. In fact the whole thing suddenly seemed like a soap opera. It seemed like the stuff Tony had been going through over the last couple of weeks, and I didn't want to act like he had.

In that instant I began to understand what Mom had told me about relationships. Everything got so complicated when you started dating. I didn't want to fight over whom I did or didn't slow-dance with or whether it was okay to talk to one girl when you were going out with another. I didn't want to get stuck in some note-passing, hallway-glaring, second-guessing junior high melodrama triangle. I didn't want to have to worry about any of that stuff. I wanted things to be the way they were when Serena and I were just goofing around, doing our algebra. I tried to tell Serena this.

"I think we should just be friends," I said.

She blinked at me. "What?"

"I want to just be friends," I said again, this time feeling more confident about it.

Her eyes narrowed at me. "McKay, you are the most aggravating boy I know. We never even went out together, and now you're breaking up with me?"

"Well, no, of course not. I didn't mean it in the breaking-up sort of way."

Until that moment I'd forgotten that's what people say to each other when they break up. *I want to just be friends.* It seemed like a really absurd thing to say when usually a person means exactly the opposite. What a person means to say is, "I don't like you, and I never want to see you again. I realize any time we run into each other, you will glare at me, and every time you are forced to say my name, you will do it as though a lemon just bit your tongue." People don't want to say the truth because they want to pretend to be all nice about it, but everyone knows what that "Let's just be friends" phrase really means. Everyone, that is, except for me thirty seconds ago, when I said it.

I quickly added, "What I mean is, I really like you, and I want to be your friend. I'm afraid if we try to be anything more than that, we'll mess it up. If you're friends, you can be friends for-ever. If you're going out together, you can only be friends until you like somebody else better. I mean, look at Tony and Rachel."

Serena nodded. Her eyes were no longer narrow. I think she was beginning to understand.

I said, "I'd like to be able to talk to you without worrying about what I'm saying. You can't do that with a girlfriend."

Now Serena smiled. "McKay, *did* you ever worry about what you were saying?"

"Yes. That's why it always came out sounding so stupid."

"It didn't always sound stupid."

"I still want to teach you how to hit a ball," I said.

"I guess I'd like that." She smiled over at me. "And I'll still help you with your math. Although now that we're just friends, I can tell you that I don't care about your baseball card collec-tion. It's just a bunch of guys in uniforms to me."

"I think horses are all right," I said, "but I've only ridden a couple of times, and both of those were the kind of things where someone leads you around with a rope."

"I'll teach you how to really ride. You'll love it."

"And I'm sure Coach Manetti will love it too. That's just what my leg needs: horseback riding lessons."

And then both of us laughed. I'm not sure at what. I guess at ourselves. She said, "Maybe being friends will be okay."

"Better than okay," I said, and suddenly I could see how it would be in the future. I saw us sitting in class and doing home-work together. I saw us talking in the school hallways, and I saw her cheering for me at school baseball games. Serena would go through a dozen and a half Brians, and I'd be there to sympathize with her when it didn't work out. And maybe someday, down the road, we would become boyfriend and girlfriend, and that would be okay too because we'd been friends first.

Serena and I talked for another half an hour, and then she said she had to go because it was about dinnertime. She smiled when she got up. "I'll bring you your algebra homework if you want."

"Thanks. Are you still going to watch me play baseball?"

"Sure. I'll be there for every quarter."

"Inning," I told her. "Football has quarters. Baseball has innings."

"Whatever." She grinned. "I'll be there for all of them."

She said good-bye, and I watched her leave. You know, it's strange how your mood can change so easily. I never would have thought that a peanut butter and mustard sandwich and a bouquet of lantana would have made me so happy, but they did. Even though my ankle was still swollen, hurting, and purple and green, I felt better. So I guess, in a way, my miracle happened after all.

I sat out for game five, but I could hobble around well enough when it was time for game six that Coach Manetti said I could bat. Serena was there watching. In fact, she'd dragged Brian along with her. As I recall, he never cheered very loudly. He also wished me good luck with a stiff and pained smile on his face. I would have liked to think this was because he was tormented with guilt for his part in my injury, but he was probably just mad Serena had made him come to watch me.

Anna also came to the game, although she didn't sit anywhere near Serena. She brought another one of her friends, Krissy, and they sat up front and completely ignored the game except for when Tony went to bat. Then they clapped and hollered. Krissy clapped especially loud, and I wondered if she was a fan of the game, or just a fan of Tony's. Then I wondered why in the world Anna would bring Krissy with her to watch the game, given Tony's track record with his girlfriend's friends.

I could only bat once, late in the inning, because after the pinch runner replaced me, I wasn't allowed back into the game. But I hit the tying run in, and my replacement ended up scoring to put us ahead. It felt odd to see someone else running over home plate in my place, and even odder to sit out during my team's turn in the outfield, but it was better than sitting in the bleachers with my parents, so I didn't complain. I was still part of the team. That was enough.

We won that game, and the last tournament game too. We were undefeated. When the final inning was up, and we were officially the district winners, everyone on my team rushed onto the field, screaming and jumping around. I ran onto the field much slower, and I jumped a lot less, but I still screamed just as loud. We'd done it. We'd all done it.

Tony and I gave each other our high fives and yelled, "Who

the champion?—You the champion!—No, you the champion!"
until we were almost hoarse.

After a while my parents made it through the throng to congratulate me. "You did wonderfully," Mom said, and gave me a
hug. "How's your ankle feeling?"

"It's fine."

"Do you think you're up to attending the victory party?"
Every season, whether we had a winning record or not, Coach
Manetti held a victory party for the team at his house.

"Sure." I wasn't about to turn down an afternoon of junk
food and bragging with the rest of the team just because my
ankle hurt a little. I only worried about one thing. Family and
friends of the team members were also invited, and I knew I
ought to ask Serena if she wanted to come. I wanted her to
come, but I wasn't so thrilled about having Brian hanging
around scowling somewhere while I was trying to celebrate.

My parents congratulated me again, then told me they'd be
ready to leave in just a minute, because they had to go and talk
to some of the other kids' parents. My parents like to talk, so I
knew it would be a little while until they were ready to go. Tony
went off to talk to Anna and Krissy, and as I didn't want to have
to stand there and be a spectator at their flirt-fest, I headed
back to where most of the team was still gathered. Serena intercepted me along the way.

"Hey, you're the winner!" she said.

"You never doubted that, did you?" I looked around and
noticed she was alone. "Where's Brian?"

"He didn't come today."

It's true, I hadn't seen him in the crowd, but I assumed he was just lurking somewhere unseen. Sort of like bacteria. "He missed a good game," I said.

"I'll tell him about it."

"Don't leave out the part where I lead the team to victory with my fabulously amazing hits."

She laughed and shook her head.

"You want to come to the team's victory party?" I asked.

She shrugged. "Sure."

We walked together over to where the team was. I took a deep breath of the cool afternoon air and smiled just because life was so great. All in all, it was a pretty good ending to the game.